DOCTOR WHO
THE MIND OF EVIL

DOCTOR WHO
THE MIND OF EVIL

Based on the BBC television serial by Don Houghton by arrangement with the British Broadcasting Corporation

Terrance Dicks

Number 96
in the
Doctor Who Library

A TARGET BOOK

published by
the Paperback Division of
W. H. ALLEN & Co. PLC

A Target Book
Published in 1985
By the Paperback Division of
W. H. Allen & Co. PLC
44 Hill Street, London W1X 8LB

First published in Great Britain by
W. H. Allen & Co. PLC in 1985

The BBC producer of *The Mind of Evil* was Barry Letts, the director was
Timothy Combe.

Printed and bound in Great Britain by
Anchor Brendon Limited, Tiptree, Essex

ISBN 0 426 20166 3

1

The Sentence

The prisoners always knew when sentence was to be carried out. They had known in the savage days when the condemned man was paraded in state to Tyburn Tree, there to meet his fate before a cheering, roaring mob of bloodthirsty spectators.

They had known in the later, relatively more civilised years, when dazed, pale-faced men were marched across the prison yard to the execution shed, to end their lives before prison governor, chaplain, and a few grim-faced warders.

And they knew today.

Tyburn Tree and the silent scaffold were things of the past, but still, somewhere in the prison, one of their number waited in the condemned cell, waited for the sound of marching footsteps in the corridor and the flinging open of the cell door.

The prisoners knew, and they reacted as they had always reacted, muttering and cursing and shouting, and rattling tin cups and plates against the bars of their cells.

As the hour when sentence was to be executed drew closer the sound rose in volume and intensity, like the mindless shriek of some great beast.

Sentence was about to be carried out on George Patrick Barnham, and his fellow prisoners were paying him the traditional tribute.

* * *

Looking incongruously bright and cheerful, the little yellow Edwardian roadster drove surprisingly quickly up the steep hill towards the grimly louring bulk of Stangmoor Prison.

The man driving the car was almost as unusual as his vehicle. He was tall and thin and beaky nosed with a lined young-old face and a mane of prematurely white hair. He wore a ruffled shirt, an elegant burgundy smoking jacket and a flowing cloak. Beside him sat a very small, very pretty fair-haired girl in a brown leather trouser suit and roll-necked sweater.

The tall man was that once-wandering Time Lord known only as the Doctor, now exiled to the planet Earth by the all-powerful rulers of his race. The Doctor was currently serving as Unpaid Scientific Adviser to an organisation called UNIT. The girl was his assistant: her name was Jo Grant.

The car came to a sudden halt outside the main gate. Jo Grant looked up at the gloomy bulk of the huge old building and shuddered. 'It looks like Dracula's Castle!'

The Doctor swung his long legs over the side of the car. 'Well, you're right about the castle bit, anyway. It used to be a fortress in the Middle Ages.' He jabbed a thumb at the old-fashioned bell-push.

Jo jumped out of the car. 'Doctor, you'll need these. You'd better keep yours on you.'

She handed him a couple of security passes. Despite his new status as a member of a top secret organisation, the Doctor hated carrying passes, papers and identification permits, and usually left that side of things to Jo. She sometimes thought that a large part of her job was to stop the Doctor from getting arrested for poking his nose into places where he had no official business.

'Thanks, Jo,' said the Doctor resignedly. Glancing keenly about him, he saw the incongruous shape of a remote control TV camera fixed to the old stone walls above the massive door. 'Smile, Jo!'

'What?'

The Doctor pointed upwards. 'You're on camera!' Gazing up at the lens, the Doctor bowed, waved and smiled.

In the security room just inside the prison an amazed guard stared at the extraordinary figure on his monitor screen. Flicking a switch, he despatched the gate guard to see what was going on.

The Doctor was still waving and smiling when the door swung open to reveal a prison officer staring impassively at him.

The Doctor smiled, a little sheepishly. 'Oh, good morning! Observers from UNIT.' He proffered the passes.

The prison officer took them, studied them, looked hard at the Doctor and Jo and then up at the camera. 'Right. Passes checked and satisfactory. Open the gates.'

He handed back the passes, the gate swung open and the Doctor and Jo got back into Bessie and drove along a ring road, through a second check-point, and on into the inner courtyard of Stangmoor Prison.

Jo couldn't help shuddering as they went into the main prison building and the metal doors clanged shut behind them. There was something horrifying about the grim old prison. She was very glad she was only there on a visit . . .

In the main prison area, the din was appalling now. Senior Prison Officer Powers, a burly craggy-faced man, strode grimly along the echoing corridors to where a group of his colleagues stood waiting. 'All right, Mr Green, let's get them quieted down. The Governor's on his way.'

9

Green and the others moved along the corridors, hammering on cell doors, ordering the prisoners to stop the noise. They had very little effect.

Three men came striding along the corridor of the Special Wing. In the lead was Victor Camford, the Prison Governor, a massive, heavy-featured man with dark hair and bushy eyebrows. Beside him was the elegant, dark-suited figure of Professor Kettering, looking as if he was about to attend an appointment at his Harley Street consulting rooms. The third man wore a white coat, thinning hair and a permanently worried expression. This was Roland Summers, the Prison Doctor.

The banging and shouting seemed to follow them along the corridor.

Kettering winced and glanced irritably at Dr Summers. 'Why do they have to make that dreadful row?'

'Tradition, Professor Kettering. Always happens when sentence is about to be carried out.'

By now the little party had reached the door of the cell at the end of the corridor. Powers produced his keys, unlocked the door, and stood back so that the Governor and his companions could go inside.

The cell was larger than most, light and airy. It was better furnished too, with a proper bed, a table and some reasonably comfortable chairs.

A man lay motionless on the bed, staring up at the ceiling. A massive brute of a man with a low bulging forehead, protruding jaw and huge powerful hands. Those hands had once choked the life out of a security guard who had been unwise enough to disturb Barnham while he was blowing a safe. They had throttled a fellow prisoner in a dispute over a cigarette, and half-strangled a prison officer.

Barnham was immensely strong, naturally ferocious,

10

and completely without scruples of any kind – qualities that had led him inevitably to the cell he now occupied.

The condemned cell.

Two warders Johnson and Samuels, sat at the table beside the bed, a pack of cards between them. Johnson, the older man, looked at Barnham. 'Care for a game?'

Barnham's lips twisted. 'Get lost.'

'Suit yourself.'

The warder started to deal the cards. Suddenly the cell door was flung open. The Governor appeared in the doorway, Kettering and Doctor Summers behind him.

Barnham tensed as the Governor stepped into the cell.

'George Patrick Barnham . . .'

With an animal-like spring, Barnham was on his feet, crouched on the other side of the bed. 'Get away from me!'

The Governor said, 'You have been sentenced by a Court of Law . . .'

'Get away,' screamed Barnham. 'You're not taking me anywhere!'

The Governor continued with the ritual pronouncement. 'The time has now come for that sentence to be carried out . . .'

Barnham glared wildly at him. 'No! Get out, the lot of you!'

'Look,' muttered Doctor Summers, 'I'd better give him something to calm him . . .'

But Barnham heard him. 'You'll give me nothing. Get away from me!'

Chief Officer Powers stepped forward. 'Now pack it in, Barnham. You're just being stupid.'

While he distracted Barnham's attention, the two other warders began edging into position behind the frantic prisoner.

'You're not taking me out of here!' shrieked Barnham.

'All right,' said Powers briefly. 'Get him.'

The warders leaped forwards, catching Barnham in a double arm-lock.

He began struggling furiously, heaving the two men from side to side. 'Get your lousy hands off me!'

At a nod from the Governor, Doctor Summers came forward with a hypodermic . . .

Somehow he managed to inject the furiously-struggling Barnham, though such was the man's strength that he resisted the effects of the drug for several minutes. At last the frantic struggles weakened.

'All right,' said the Governor. 'Take him away.'

Accompanied by a chorus of howls and rattling from his fellow inmates, the now semi-conscious Barnham was half-led, half-carried down the corridor.

In the room called the Process Chamber everything was ready. It was a large, modern-looking room, quite different in atmosphere from the rest of the prison. Two large skylight-type windows were set into the vaulted roof and the whole place had a rather clinical look, like a room in a modern hospital. At one end of the room was a raised dais upon which stood what looked very much like a dentist's chair. Suspended above the chair on a flexible metal arm there was a transparent dome. Chair and dome were connected to a strange-looking machine which stood on a glass table close by.

The base of the machine was low and flat and square, its shape not unlike that of a video-recorder. Rising from the flat base was an opaque central column, short and wide with a sort of black dome on the top. There were dials and meters set into a panel in the front of the base. The whole device was connected in turn to an elaborate control console that stood against the nearby wall.

In front of the extraordinary set-up there were several rows of chairs. Scattered about the room was a little group of waiting observers, who had been listening with mounting uneasiness to the appalling din from outside, which was only now beginning to die down.

A stern-looking man in the uniform of Senior Prison Officer strode into the room. 'All right, ladies and gentlemen, there's nothing to worry about, just a temporary disturbance. If you'll take your seats please . . .'

The Doctor led Jo to a couple of seats in the centre of the front row. He had never suffered from false modesty.

'Temporary disturbance indeed,' whispered Jo. 'Sounded more like a full scale riot to me.'

The Doctor nodded, settled himself in his chair, and gazed disapprovingly round at his fellow-observers, a motley collection of policemen, medical students and civil servants.

'Morbid lot of sensation seekers,' he muttered.

Jo gave him a look. 'Why did you insist on coming?'

'Scientific curiosity,' said the Doctor with an air of offended dignity.

'Oh, yes?'

'Yes. Something's been worrying me about this Keller process ever since I first heard about it.' He broke off as two men came into the room. 'I think the curtain is about to go up!'

The Governor cleared his throat. 'Good morning, ladies and gentlemen!'

There was the usual embarrassed mutter from everyone except the Doctor who said, 'Good morning!' in a loud clear voice.

Giving him a rather surprised look the Governor went on. 'Ladies and gentlemen, may I introduce Professor Kettering, who will explain the process you are now about to see demonstrated.'

Thankfully the Governor stood aside, leaving the centre of the stage to Kettering, who stepped forward, addressing his audience with the confidence of an experienced lecturer.

13

'Today, ladies and gentlemen, we no longer execute even the most hardened criminals and killers. Society has progressed far beyond that primitive form of retribution.'

'All depends what you mean by progress, doesn't it?' said the Doctor audibly.

Kettering shot him a quelling look, and there was a disapproving murmur from the respectful audience.

'Today,' continued Kettering, 'science has abolished the hangman's noose and substituted *this* infallible method.' He gestured towards the machine.

Once again the Doctor's voice was perfectly audible. 'People who talk about infallibility are usually on very shaky ground!'

Kettering glared at him and raised his voice. 'For the benefit of the less sophisticated members of my audience I will explain the process in very simple terms. Professor Emil Keller, the inventor of this process, discovered that anti-social behaviour was governed by certain negative or 'evil' impulses. This machine, the Keller Machine, isolates and extracts these impulses, leaving a rational, well-balanced individual.'

'I bet it doesn't!' This was the Doctor again.

'May I continue?' said Kettering.

The Doctor nodded affably. 'By all means!'

'Thank you.' Kettering moved over to the machine. 'The condemned man is placed in this chair with his head beneath this dome. A series of probes are attached to his skull, so as to connect with the neural circuits.' He moved over to the console. 'The extraction process is controlled from this console here, and the negative impulses are stored in what we refer to as the reservoir box at the base of the machine.'

'Where do they go after that?' asked the Doctor.

'Nowhere, sir. I repeat, they are stored in the box.'

'Which, presumably, is full of your negative or evil impulses?'

14

Kettering gave him a patronising smile. 'Not full. The indicator registers only sixty-five per cent at the present time – and the machine has already been used very successfully in Switzerland, in the processing of one hundred and twelve cases. This will be the one hundred and thirteenth.' He stepped back. 'Doctor Summers!'

Two warders wheeled in a trolley upon which lay the body of a huge brutal-looking man in prison clothing. They lifted him from the trolley and settled him in the chair. Summers lowered the helmet over his head and began connecting the necessary electrodes.

'When this process is finished,' said Kettering impressively, 'the negative impulses which made this man a criminal will have been removed. He will take his place as a useful, if lowly, member of society. If you are ready, Doctor Summers?'

Summers nodded.

The prisoner lolled back in the chair staring dazedly ahead of him, his face half-concealed by the transparent dome.

Kettering moved to the console. His hands moved over the controls and the machine began humming with power.

The lights in the Process Chamber dimmed.

The power build-up continued, and dials on the console began climbing steadily. The machine began giving out a regular pulsing, a high-pitched electronic sound, curiously like the scream of an animal.

Jo Grant watched the macabre scene in horrified fascination. It *wasn't* an execution, of course, yet somehow it felt like one. And no doubt curing people was much better than killing them – yet somehow what was happening felt *wrong*. There was an atmosphere of gloating evil in the room, and it was connected in Jo's mind with the squat shape of the Keller Machine. She couldn't rid herself of the idea that there was something

15

malignant and alive inside that stubby central column, and that it was *growing* . . .

The hum of power grew louder, the electronic pulse increased . . . Suddenly Barnham shrieked loudly, arching his back in agony.

'What's happening Doctor?' whispered Jo.

'I don't know. But there's something evil about that machine,' said the Doctor, echoing Jo's thoughts.

Kettering was busy at the console, switching off the machine.

Doctor Summers was anxiously checking Barnham's pulse and respiration. He glanced at the central dial on the front of the machine. 'Look at the dial, Professor Kettering.'

Kettering looked. The dial showed a massive increase in negative impulses.

The Governor whispered, 'Professor Kettering, what's happening?'

Kettering raised his voice, addressing not only the Governor but the audience. 'There was a minor malfunction, but the machine compensated. The process is now complete . . .' Kettering looked quickly at Summers, who looked up from his examination and nodded. At least the man was still alive.

'The process is completed – satisfactorily,' Kettering said loudly.

'Satisfactorily be blowed,' said the Doctor indignantly.

Kettering waved to the warders, who lifted Barnham from the chair, returned him to the trolley, and wheeled him away.

'The subject will now be taken away to recuperate. Within an hour or two he will be perfectly normal.'

'I admire your confidence, sir,' said the Doctor.

'Thank you,' said Kettering blandly. 'That is all, gentlemen.'

The audience began drifting away.

16

Kettering went to join the Governor, who looked uneasily at him. 'I take it everything *was* all right Professor Kettering?'

'Of course, Governor.'

A third voice said, 'Then perhaps you can explain that unfortunate man's reaction?'

Kettering turned and saw that his odd-looking interrupter had followed him.

'An excess of negative particles – the machine overreacted, and then corrected itself.'

'In other words – you don't know?'

'May I ask who you are, sir?'

The Governor said, 'The Doctor is Scientific Adviser to UNIT – the United Nations Intelligence Taskforce.'

'How interesting,' said Kettering. 'Though I really don't see what concern this is of theirs.'

The Doctor was more than happy to enlighten him. 'UNIT, sir, was formed to deal with new and unusual menaces to mankind. In my view, that machine of yours is precisely that!'

George Patrick Barnham lay in a hospital bed in one of the rooms in the Medical Wing, sleeping peacefully, and apparently quite undisturbed by Doctor Summers's examination.

Professor Kettering strode into the room, still seething from his encounter with the Doctor. 'Well? How is he?'

'Nothing much wrong with him physically. Respiration normal. Pulse rate a little high, but I gather that's normal after the process.'

'Exactly!' said Kettering with satisfaction. 'A completely successful treatment.'

'The reaction was extremely violent,' said Summers doubtfully.

'Really, my dear Summers, you're as bad as that interfering fool from UNIT!'

17

The wall telephone rang, and Summers lifted the receiver. 'Medical Wing?' He listened for a moment, in mounting agitation. 'Have you told the Governor? I'll be right over.' Doctor Summers signalled a medical orderly. 'Stay here and keep an eye on him. Professor Kettering, you'd better come with me.'

'Is anything the matter?'

'There's been some kind of accident in the Process Chamber. a man's been hurt. They think he's dead.'

2

The Terror

Doctor Summers hurried into the Process Chamber to find Chief Prison Officer Green standing guard over a huddled shape on the floor.

Summers knelt to examine the body. 'Who is he?'

Green shook his head. 'No idea, sir.'

The Governor came in, the Doctor and Jo close behind him.

'What happened, Green?'

'I don't know, sir. I was coming along the corridor to check that everyone was gone, and I heard him screaming . . .'

The Doctor looked down at Summers. 'Is he dead?'

'Yes, he's dead.'

The Doctor knelt to examine the body for a moment, and then straightened up.

'Probably a heart attack,' said Kettering uneasily. 'Delayed shock from seeing the Process.'

'Perhaps,' said the Doctor briskly. 'But I doubt it.' He turned to Doctor Summers, taking charge as usual. 'Might I suggest an immediate post mortem – and an investigation into his past medical history?'

'Yes . . . yes, an excellent idea!' said Summers a little bemusedly. 'I'll see to it right away.'

Remembering she was supposed to be a trained UNIT operative, Jo conquered her natural squeamishness and examined the body. 'Doctor?'

'What is it, Jo?'

'Look at his face. He looks terrified. And those marks – like. . .'

'Bites or scratches, Jo? Yes, I know . . .'

'Hadn't we better report this to the Brigadier?'

'I quite agree, Jo, but not yet. Let's wait for the results of that post mortem, then I'll have more to go on.'

'All right. Anyway, I suppose the Brigadier wouldn't thank us for disturbing him right now.'

The Doctor was staring abstractedly at the Keller machine. 'Mmm?'

'You know, Doctor. The Peace Conference. UNIT is in charge of Security.'

UNIT's new HQ was converted from a big old house in a pleasant London square. In his office, a large and airy room with a view over London's rooftops, Brigadier Alastair Lethbridge-Stewart, commanding officer of the British branch of UNIT, was on the telephone to the Minister. The Brigadier was being politely mutinous. 'That's all very well, sir, but in my opinion – '

He broke off, interrupted by the insistent voice on the other end of the phone. 'Yes, yes, I see. I take it that is your final decision? Very well, sir.' With controlled fury, the Brigadier put down the phone.

Captain Yates, the Brigadier's second-in-command came into the room in time to hear the end of the conversation. Mike Yates was a thin, sensitive-looking young man, a good deal tougher than he looked. 'Trouble, sir?'

'That was the Minister. UNIT *will* accept responsibility for the safe transport of the Thunderbolt Missile. It's been cleared with Geneva.'

'That's all we needed, sir – with the Peace Conference on our hands as well.'

The Brigadier stood up. 'I want you to take charge of

20

the escort detail, Captain Yates. I've got too much on my plate as it is.'

If Mike Yates resented being diverted to a difficult and potentially dangerous side-show he was too well trained to show it. 'I'll get on to it right away, sir.'

'Is the Doctor back from Stangmoor yet?'

'No, sir. What exactly is he doing down there?'

The Brigadier sighed. 'Observing some new development in the treatment of criminals. I suppose it'll keep him out of mischief. How are things at the Peace Conference?'

'All seems to be running pretty smoothly, sir.'

'Let's hope it lasts,' said the Brigadier gloomily.

It didn't. No sooner were the words out of his mouth than there came the sound of two angry voices from the outer office.

Both were female, and the first was that of the UNIT corporal who acted as the Brigadier's secretary and receptionist. 'I'm sorry, you can't go in. The Brigadier is very busy.'

The second voice spoke perfect text-book English, with the unmistakeable speech rhythms of the Orient. 'And I tell you that the matter is most urgent. I must see the Brigadier immediately. Out of my way!'

The Brigadier drew a deep breath, expanding his lungs for a reprimanding bellow, but before he could get the words out of his mouth, a small, grey-uniformed and very angry Chinese girl marched briskly into his office, closely followed by an indignant Corporal Bell.

The Brigadier let out his breath in a long sigh. 'All right, Corporal Bell.' He looked at the Chinese girl who was standing in front of his desk, quivering with anger. 'Yes, Captain, what can I do for you?'

It occurred to Mike Yates, as he brought forward a chair, that in her off-duty moments, if she ever had any, Captain Chin Lee of the Chinese People's Army would be a remarkably attractive girl. She was still in her mid-twenties, and the high-cheekboned face with its huge dark eyes was undeniably beautiful. But the face was marred by an almost permanent scowl of angry indignation.

Ignoring the chair, the girl stood stiffly at attention. 'Brigadier! An outrage has been committed against the Chinese People's Delegation. As you are in charge of the security arrangements, I hold you directly responsible.'

It was the accusing tone that was so objectionable, decided the Brigadier. That and the almost hysterical assumption that *every* delay, difficulty or set-back, any least thing that displeased the touchy Chinese Delegation was the result of a carefully planned Western Imperialist Conspiracy. 'What is it now, Captain Chin Lee?'

'Important State documents have been stolen from General Cheng Teik's suite.'

'That's impossible,' said Mike Yates immediately. 'There's a twenty-four hour guard on all the delegates' suites.'

'Nevertheless, the theft has occurred. Your guards are inefficient. Probably they take bribes.'

'*That is an insulting suggestion!*' The Brigadier spoke with such fury that even Chin Lee looked alarmed. With an effort he controlled himself. 'Very well, Captain, leave it with me. We shall look into the matter immediately.'

'I must warn you Brigadier that this incident puts the success of this Peace Conference in grave jeopardy. We suspect the American Imperialists of this crime.'

'Naturally,' said the Brigadier drily. His voice hardened. 'I assure you that every effort will be made to locate the missing papers and to find and punish whoever is responsible.'

'If there is any further trouble, our Delegation will

withdraw from this conference.' With this parting shot, Captain Chin Lee turned and marched out of the office.

Gloomily, the Brigadier watched her go. 'More trouble!'

'Mmm,' said Mike Yates thoughtfully. 'Pity. She's quite a dolly.'

Catching the Brigadier's eye, Mike returned hurriedly to his duties.

Filled with a virtuous glow that came from the knowledge of having done her duty, Captain Chin Lee strode out of UNIT HQ and stood for a moment on the steps, looking out at the pleasant London square. Children were playing in the garden in the centre. The sounds of their laughter drifted across to her.

Suddenly she became aware that there was something else she had to do. Something else . . .

Her official limousine was parked outside the building, and the chauffeur leaped forward to open the door for her. Blank-faced, Chin Lee walked straight past him, crossed the road and walked through the little garden.

At a secluded spot on the far side she paused beside a wire litter bin and took a sheaf of important-looking papers from inside her tunic. The papers bore the seal of the Chinese Delegation. Producing a big, old-fashioned cigarette lighter from her tunic pocket, Captain Chin Lee set fire to the papers, holding them up by one corner.

A strange electronic pulsing filled her mind, and she fingered the metal disc high on her neck, hidden by her hair . . . Only when the yellow flames were licking at her fingers did she drop the remnants of the papers into the bin and turn away.

As she walked back to her car, her face was calm and placid. Already it was as if the incident had completely faded from her mind.

* * *

The throbbing of the Keller Machine was dying away as Jo Grant, the Doctor, Professor Kettering and the Prison Governor hurried into the Process Chamber.

The Doctor turned angrily to Kettering. 'Do you still insist this Process is working normally?'

'Of course it is,' said Kettering defensively. 'I mean, you've just seen Barnham, haven't you?'

The Doctor nodded, but it was clear from his expression that he was far from convinced.

'Look here,' continued Kettering. 'Emil Keller himself installed the machine here. I worked very closely with him. I know every facet of the process.'

The Doctor stared gloomily down at the console. 'I don't like it, Governor, I never did.'

'Don't like what?'

'Interfering with the powers of the mind. It's a dangerous business.'

Kettering said furiously, 'All this is hardly your concern, Doctor.'

'Professor Kettering, it is *everyone's* concern!'

They were interrupted by the entrance of Doctor Summers, looking, if possible, even more worried than usual.

The Governor turned to him with relief. 'Ah, Doctor Summers! Any news for us?'

Summers nodded. 'I've got the post-mortem report here.' Fussily he looked through a sheaf of papers. 'The deceased's name was Arthur Linwood, he was a medical student in his final year . . .'

'Yes, yes,' interrupted the Doctor. 'But what did he die of?'

'Heart failure.'

Kettering gave a sigh of relief. 'There you are then. The strain of watching the Process was too much for him.'

Doctor Summers said slowly, 'But he didn't *have* a weak heart, Professor Kettering.'

24

'*Anything* unusual in his medical history?' asked the Doctor.

Summers nodded. 'I called his Teaching Hospital. There *was* just one thing . . . Apparently he suffered from a morbid fear of certain animals. When he was working in the laboratory, he was absolutely terrified of – '

'Rats?' suggested the Doctor.

Summers looked at him in surprise. 'Yes.'

'And those scratch marks on his neck and face - could they have been made by rats?'

'Yes, they could.'

'There are no rats in this room,' said the Governor indignantly. 'None in the entire prison, come to that.'

Summers looked up from the report. 'But all the indications are that he was attacked by a horde of them – and the shock killed him.'

'You must be mistaken,' said Kettering impatiently.

The Doctor said gently, 'But Linwood is dead.'

'Because of heart failure.'

'No. Because of this Machine.'

'I tell you the man's death had nothing to do with the Machine. If you were any sort of a scientist, my dear chap, you'd understand.'

For a moment, Jo thought the Doctor was going to explode.

'If *I* were a scientist? Let me inform you, sir, that I *am* a scientist, and have been for many thousand – '

Realising that this claim was unlikely to increase his credibility, the Doctor bit off his own words. 'Jo!' he called, and turned and stalked from the room.

'The man's mad,' said Kettering dismissively.

Jo Grant paused in the doorway. 'On the contrary, he happens to be a genius. I wish you'd listen to him, Governor.' She followed the Doctor from the room.

Doctor Summers was thoroughly bemused. 'What do you think we ought to do?'

'I think you'd better give that Machine a thorough check, Professor Kettering,' said the Governor firmly.

'Yes, of course, Governor. But I assure you, there's no cause for anxiety.'

'All the same – better safe than sorry, eh?'

With this undeniable if unoriginal sentiment the Governor left the Chamber. Doctor Summers hurried after him.

Left alone with the Machine, Professor Kettering stared uneasily at it for a moment, and then began checking the readings on the console.

The Machine hummed a little, and the dial on its base quivered . . .

All was bustle and activity in UNIT's outer office. Mike Yates was sticking pins into a giant wall map of Southern England, talking into the telephone at the same time.

Corporal Bell was on the phone as well. She looked up as the Brigadier entered the room. 'Call for you, sir.'

'Thank you, Corporal Bell. I'll take it in my office.'

As he went through to the inner office, the Brigadier heard Mike Yates saying impatiently, 'I'll give you the final security schedules just as soon as I've cleared them with the Brigadier. I'll be phoning you back within the next hour . . .'

Clearly, Yates hadn't lost any time in getting to grips with the nerve-gas Missile problem, thought the Brigadier approvingly.

He went into his office and picked up the phone. 'Lethbridge-Stewart . . . Yes, I see. You're sure? Very well, continue the search.' The Brigadier paused for a moment, then pressed a buzzer.

A moment later, Mike Yates bustled in, 'Sir?'

The Brigadier nodded towards a chair. 'Sit down.'

Mike sat down and the Brigadier continued: 'Still no trace of Chin Lee's missing papers. Our people have turned the whole place inside out. No gaps in the security system either. It wouldn't surprise me if she took the papers herself, just to cause me trouble.'

Corporal Bell put her head round the door. 'Excuse me, sir, Captain Chin Lee's on the phone.'

The Brigadier groaned.

Tactfully, Corporal Bell went on, 'Do you want me to say you're not – '

He shook his head impatiently. 'No, no, I'll speak to her.'

Corporal Bell disappeared. The Brigadier looked gloomily at Mike Yates. 'I wonder what she's complaining of this time?' The red phone buzzed, and the Brigadier picked it up. 'Good afternoon, Captain Chin Lee. How can I help – ' The Brigadier broke off, an expression of sudden concern on his face. 'Yes . . . yes, I see. Don't touch anything. I'll be over at once.' He slammed down the phone and jumped to his feet.

Mike Yates rose too. 'More stolen papers, sir?'

The Brigadier flicked the switch on his intercom. 'Get my car ready. Right away!' He turned to Mike. 'We've got real trouble now, Captain Yates. The Chinese delegate is dead!'

3

The Inferno

Professor Kettering was checking on the Keller Machine – as far as he was able, which wasn't, in fact, very far.

The truth of the matter was, he didn't understand how the Machine worked, and never had. Professor Kettering was the kind of scientist who owes his position more to a polished convincing manner, a talent for political intrigue, and the ability to charm and flatter those in positions of power, than to any real scientific ability.

Conscious as he was of the hollowness of his scientific pretensions, Kettering had been flattered and delighted when Emil Keller had chosen him to oversee the first use of the Keller Machine in England. Eager for the reflected glory, Kettering had acted as Keller's sponsor, using all his considerable influence to secure the acceptance of the Keller Process by the Government, at least on an experimental basis. He had finally convinced them to set up a trial experiment, here at Stangmoor Prison.

Of course, Emil Keller *had* explained how the Machine worked . . . But somehow the explanation was never really clear in Kettering's mind. He could remember only a low hypnotic voice, painting glowing pictures of the scientific distinctions to come, a knighthood, a peerage, perhaps even a Nobel prize.

So far Kettering had succeeded in concealing his ignorance with a good deal of high-flown scientific gobbledegook. Now things had suddenly gone terrifyingly wrong. To make matters worse, this Doctor fellow was poking around asking awkward questions – of a kind that Kettering was quite unable to answer. With steadily mounting unease, Professor Kettering went on going through the motions.

Suddenly the Keller Machine began throbbing with power . . . The electronic pulsing began . . .

Kettering looked at the Machine in astonishment. He hadn't switched it on, hadn't even touched the power switch.

Loosening his tie, Kettering began adjusting the controls, trying to shut off the Machine . . .

Shouts and yells were echoing along the corridors of the prison, tin plates and cups being rattled against the bars.

Chief Prison Officer Powers hurried onto the scene, and found his colleagues vainly trying to quell the noise.

'Starting up again, are they?' said Powers grimly. He added his powerful voice to those of the others. 'All right, now, quieten down there. Let's keep it down!'

But the prisoners took no notice. Something was stirring them up.

There was something familiar in the atmosphere, and suddenly Powers realised.

It was like Barnham's 'execution' all over again . . .

Kettering worked desperately at the controls, but it wasn't the slightest use. The Machine ignored him, as if it had a life of its own.

The weird electronic pulsing rose higher, higher . . .

Suddenly Kettering became aware that water was flowing under the door, and pouring down the walls, flooding across the floor . . .

The room was filling up with water, green billowing waves of it . . .

Kettering screamed. He had always been afraid of

water, ever since he had nearly drowned in a boating accident when he was still a child. Even now he still couldn't swim, couldn't so much as get into a boat . . .

He screamed again as the cold waves rose over his head, choking him.

Kettering drowned.

As the Doctor and Jo hurried into the Process Chamber, Doctor Summers looked up from Kettering's body. 'He's dead.'

'Dead?' repeated the Governor. 'Do you know what happened?'

Summers shook his head. 'I'm not sure . . . it seems as if . . . but it's incredible . . .'

'Come on, man,' snapped the Doctor.

'Well, from the appearance of the body, the tinge of the skin and so on – ' Summers took a deep breath. 'All the symptoms are consistent with death by drowning.'

The Governor gazed around the perfectly dry room. 'That's ridiculous, impossible.'

'Like the rats,' said the Doctor thoughtfully.

Summers looked worriedly at him. 'I think I'll go and check on Kettering's medical records.'

'Good idea,' agreed the Doctor. 'How long would you say he's been dead?'

'Matter of minutes. Five at the outside.'

Jo looked at the Doctor. 'That must be about when the riot started.'

'Exactly, Jo.'

The Governor said incredulously, 'Are you suggesting there's some connection?'

The Doctor pointed accusingly at the squat shape of the Machine. 'This – thing has the power to affect men's minds – and it's growing stronger.'

'Come now, Doctor,' said the Governor uneasily. 'It's only a machine.'

30

'Maybe and maybe not. Whatever it is, it's dangerous, and it's got to be destroyed – now.'

'I've no authority to do that. Naturally, I'll report your recommendations to the Home Office, Doctor. They'll have to decide.'

The Doctor said grimly. 'I see. I wonder how many more deaths it will take to convince them?'

The Peace Conference had taken over one of London's most exclusive luxury hotels. For the period of the conference, the entire hotel would be occupied by the delegates, their aides and secretarial staff, and members of the security services of the countries involved. UNIT had overall responsibility for the security of the conference and the safety of the delegates.

And UNIT had failed, thought the Brigadier, as he stared down at the crumpled body of General Cheng Teik. No marks on the body, an expression of unbearable terror on the face, and that was all.

Someone, or something, had broken through an impenetrable wall of security and killed the General, endangering not only the success of the Conference, but the peace of the entire world.

The accusing voice of Chin Lee broke in on his thoughts. 'First theft, then murder, Brigadier. What are you going to do about it?'

The Brigadier looked thoughtfully down at her. 'Who else knows about this?'

'No one. I called you at once.'

Mike Yates murmured, 'Should I call the police, sir?'

'Just a courtesy call. Tell them we'll handle this ourselves. I want a full check on movements in and out of this suite, Captain Yates, before and after the General's death. And no Press! D Notices!'

'Right, sir.'

As Yates moved away, the Brigadier called, 'And then

go and get the Doctor back from Stangmoor. I want him here!' He turned to Chin Lee, who was standing stiffly before him, the black eyes glaring accusingly.

'Now, Captain,' said the Brigadier, 'I'd like to know exactly what happened – in detail, please.'

'My appointment with the General was at twelve p.m. There were some details to discuss about the Conference.'

'And you were punctual?'

'I am always punctual, Brigadier. I showed my pass to your UNIT sentry and entered the General's suite as the clock was striking twelve.'

'Go on.'

'There is nothing more to say. I saw the General's body, and telephoned you.'

'Immediately?'

'Of course.'

The Brigadier glanced at his watch. 'Excuse me a moment, Captain.' He turned to Corporal Bell, who was hovering nearby and said quietly, 'I want you to check on the precise time of Captain Chin Lee's phone call.'

The Doctor and the Governor had been arguing for some time, but the Governor refused to budge. 'I'm sorry, Doctor, that's my final word. I'll suspend any further use of the Keller Process and I'll put this room out of bounds. But that's all I can do without higher authority.'

Reluctantly, the Doctor accepted defeat. 'All right. Then I'd better do what I can to make this Machine safe.' The Doctor tossed his cloak over a chair.

'I'll help, Doctor,' volunteered Jo.

'I'll do it on my own.'

'Is that wise?' asked the Governor.

'Perhaps not, but I prefer to work that way. How long has this Machine been installed?'

'Nearly a year. Emil Keller himself came over to supervise the installation.'

32

For no particular reason, the Doctor asked, 'Did he have anyone with him? An assistant?'

'Actually he did. A rather attractive Chinese girl . . .'

The atmosphere in the Chinese delegate's suite was heavy with tension as Corporal Bell put down the telephone, scribbled a note on a pad and handed it to the Brigadier.

He studied it, then looked up. 'Captain Chin Lee, you say you phoned me at twelve – immediately you discovered the body?'

'Of course.'

The Brigadier shook his head. 'No, Captain, you telephoned me at twelve-fourteen exactly.'

'You must be mistaken.'

'You called on a security line, Captain. All security calls are logged.'

Chin Lee was silent.

'Well?' demanded the Brigadier. 'Why did you wait for almost a quarter of an hour before reporting the crime?'

Despite the Doctor's orders, Jo insisted on hanging around while he checked over the Keller Machine. 'What are you doing, Doctor?'

'Hunting,' said the Doctor briefly. 'And will you please let me get on with it?'

'I'm only trying to help.'

'Yes, of course you are. Look, why don't you go along and see if Doctor Summers has got any more information about Kettering's death?'

'Right. I'll bring it straight back here.'

'No!' said the Doctor hurriedly. 'Take it to the Governor's office. I'll meet you there later.'

'Okay!' Reluctantly Jo headed for the door.

'Well, off you go then.'

33

Jo turned away, but she couldn't resist turning in the doorway, for a final look at what the Doctor was doing.

Without turning round the Doctor shouted, 'Boo!'

Jo jumped, and scurried from the room.

She found Doctor Summers in the medical wing, and passed on the Doctor's request.

Summers pointed to a pile of papers on the table. 'I've just got the post mortem report.'

'What's the verdict?'

'Kettering's lungs were full of water. He drowned – in the middle of a perfectly dry room.'

The banging and yelling had begun again in the corridors of the prison. 'They suddenly started up, Chief,' said Prison Officer Green helplessly. 'Just like the other times.'

'All right. Let's get them quieted down, shall we?'

Powers and Green and all the other warders moved along the corridors, admonishing, cajoling, threatening. 'All right, now, all right! Quieten down, will you? Quieten down!' But it was no use.

The noise became an angry roar.

The Doctor heard the distant sounds and looked up uneasily from his task. He was working under a sense of increasing strain, though he didn't quite know why.

The Machine began to throb, slowly at first, then louder, and then there came a strange electronic pulsing.

It was unbearably hot.

Loosening his collar, the Doctor went on with his work.

There was something nagging at the back of his mind. Something about the Keller Machine. No, not about the Machine, but about something *like* it . . . something dangerous and evil.

The Doctor's Time Lord superiors had blocked off his memory of Time Travel theory when they exiled him to Earth. Unfortunately, other areas of memory had been affected as well. The information was there, somewhere, but he couldn't reach it.

The Doctor became aware that the electronic pulsing was very much louder.

The Keller Machine caught fire.

Tendrils of flame leaped up from its base, shooting upwards, turning the Machine into a roaring fireball.

Floor and ceiling suddenly burst into flames. Rivers of glowing lava poured down the walls.

The Doctor was trapped – in the centre of a blazing inferno . . .

4

The Listener

Driven back by the unbearable searing heat, the Doctor flailed wildly about him, as if trying to drive back the flames with his bare hands. He was crouched in one corner, about to be engulfed – when Jo Grant came into the room, some papers in her hand.

To her astonishment she saw the Doctor lashing out wildly at the empty air. The room was filled with a strange electronic pulsing sound.

'Doctor!' she called. 'What's the matter? What are you doing?'

The strange sound died away.

The Doctor stared wildly at her. 'The fire,' he muttered. 'The fire . . .' Straightening up, he moved rather shakily over to a chair and collapsed into it.

Jo looked round. The room was perfectly normal. '*What* fire?'

The Doctor stared dazedly at her. 'What are you doing here, Jo?'

'You wanted that medical report on Kettering. I got it from Doctor Summers.'

'I told you to take it to the Governor's office.'

'But I thought it was important.'

'So are my instructions, Jo. You could have been killed.'

'*Me* killed?' said Jo indignantly. 'It seemed to me you

were the one in danger. You looked as if you were fighting something that wasn't there.'

'Oh, it was there, Jo, at least until you came in. Your arrival distracted it, broke its grip on my mind.' The Doctor smiled, making Jo feel she'd managed to do something right after all. 'Now, let me see that report.'

Jo handed him the report. The Doctor studied it thoughtfully.

'You were right about Kettering, Doctor. Death by drowning – he had a morbid fear of water.'

'And so he drowned – in a perfectly dry room.'

'Doctor – what did *you* see?'

'Fire, Jo.'

'But why should you – '

The Doctor was staring into space as if re-living scenes of unimaginable horror. 'Some time ago, I saw a terrible catastrophe. A whole world ended in flames.'

The Doctor was silent for a moment, thinking of Project Inferno, of the time when he had seen a parallel Earth, quite real in its own dimension, explode in smoke and flame. 'The Machine plucked that memory out of my mind, and used it to attack me.'

'This fire you saw – it wasn't real?'

'The rats weren't real or the water. Yet Linwood died, and so did Kettering. We believe what our minds tell us, Jo.'

'If Keller's Machine is so dangerous, why don't you just blow it up?'

The Doctor rose. 'Because the idiots in authority won't let me. I'm trying to work out a way of controlling it instead. Now, if you've quite finished asking questions . . .' The Doctor picked up a screwdriver and set to work.

'All right, I'm going,' said Jo hurriedly.

She was heading for the door when it opened and Captain Yates strode in. 'Mike! What are you doing here?'

The Doctor slammed down his screwdriver in disgust.

'Brigadier's orders,' said Mike crisply. 'Doctor, I'm afraid you've got to come back to London with me.'

'Nonsense. I couldn't possibly leave Stangmoor at the moment.'

'You've got to, Doctor.'

'I tell you I'm not leaving.' The Doctor turned back to his work.

Mike Yates advanced towards him. As far as he was concerned refusal to obey a lawful order was mutiny. He'd been told to bring the Doctor back and he intended to bring him. 'I'm sorry, Doctor, you're coming with me. I'm quite prepared to use force if I have to.' He grabbed the Doctor's shoulder.

The Doctor swung round, shot out a long arm, and jabbed a bony finger at a point below Mike's collar bone. That was all – but somehow Mike found that he couldn't move.

'Venusian Karate,' explained the Doctor. 'Or perhaps Venusian Aikido would be a better description. You might find using force on *me* rather more difficult than you imagine, young man!'

Mike Yates discovered that although he couldn't move, he could still talk. 'The Brigadier really does need you, Doctor,' he gasped. 'Things are in a very bad way at the Peace Conference. The Chinese Delegate's dead – we think he's been murdered.'

The Doctor released him. 'Murdered! Very well, Captain Yates, I'll come.'

Mike rubbed his shoulder. 'Thank you, Doctor.'

'That's right, Doctor, you go,' said Jo brightly. 'I'll stay down here and look after things for you.'

The Doctor groaned inwardly. The thought of leaving something as dangerous as the Keller Machine in the hands of this feather-headed child . . . Still, there was no alternative.

38

He put his hands on her shoulders. 'Jo, for once in your young life, do you think you could do just as I ask?'

'Yes, of course, Doctor.'

'Then get the Governor to lock and bar that door. No one is to come into this room. *No one.*'

'Just leave everything to me.'

The Doctor sighed. 'I'm afraid I'll have to! Try and stay out of trouble, will you?'

'Yes, Doctor,' said Jo obediently.

The Doctor swung round. 'Well, Captain Yates, what are we waiting for?' He strode from the room.

Mike Yates gave Jo a rueful look, and hurried after him. Picking up the Doctor's cloak, Jo followed, closing the door and locking it from outside.

The Keller Machine was left alone. After a moment it began to throb – very gently. It was almost as if it was biding its time.

Sergeant Benton was being James Bond.

At least, he was on plain-clothes duty for once and somewhere in the back of his mind there lurked hopeful pictures of vodka martinis, shaken but not stirred, Bentley sports cars and mysteriously beautiful international spies.

His actual assignment was considerably more routine. He was tailing Captain Chin Lee.

Since the Chinese girl had a kind of semi-diplomatic status, the Brigadier had been unable to arrest her. Instead, convinced that she had something to hide, the Brigadier had decided to have her followed when she left UNIT HQ after her interrogation.

Unfortunately, the job of protecting the Peace Conference had left him very short of manpower, and he had been forced to assign the only available man, Benton.

The Sergeant had many excellent qualities. He was a burly, handsome young man, a fine figure in his military uniform. He was completely fearless and utterly loyal. But he wouldn't have been the Brigadier's first choice for an undercover assignment.

For one thing, he was just too big. Benton lurking in a doorway with his raincoat collar turned up, was about as inconspicuous as an elephant at a tea party.

Still, he *was* lurking all the same, in a doorway behind UNIT HQ keeping an eye on Captain Chin Lee who was making a call from a public telephone box. That in itself was suspicious, thought Benton. There were plenty of phones at UNIT HQ. Why come out into the back streets to find a phone box unless you had something to hide?

Chin Lee came out of the box.

To Benton's horror she stood staring fixedly at him for a moment, obviously well aware of his presence. She touched a hand to her neck, just under her hair . . .

Suddenly a strange electronic pulsing filled Benton's mind. A sensation of terrible fear swept over him. Everything began spinning around, and he collapsed against the railings, his hands to his head . . .

Chin Lee looked impassively at the writhing figure on the pavement, hurried around the corner and disappeared.

Benton heard a voice. 'Hey, mate, you all right?' His vision cleared and he saw a concerned passer-by staring down at him.

Struggling to his feet, Benton looked around him. Chin Lee was nowhere to be seen. He sighed, thinking of the Brigadier's inevitable reaction. This sort of thing never happened to James Bond.

Crestfallen, Benton began walking back around the block to UNIT HQ.

Telephone Company engineers were working on the other side of the square. They'd put up one of those mysterious little canvas huts that seem an essential part

40

of all Telephone Company operations. Benton was so used to it that he didn't give it a second glance. He went up the steps and disappeared inside UNIT HQ.

Minutes later, Chin Lee emerged from the little hut and walked quickly away.

The Brigadier's reaction was all that Benton had feared. 'You *lost* her, Benton?'

'Yes, sir,' said Benton miserably. 'She gave me the slip. One minute I had her well in sight – and the next . . .'

'She vanished in a puff of smoke?' suggested the Brigadier witheringly.

'No, sir. I got this sort of throbbing in my head . . . I must have fainted. When I came round she was gone.'

'Throbbing in the head?' snapped the Brigadier. '*Fainted?* You're too delicate for intelligence work, Sergeant Benton. You'd better go and lie down!'

'Yes, sir. Sorry, sir.'

'Dismissed, Sergeant,' roared the Brigadier. 'Just get out of my sight!'

Benton turned and shot thankfully out of the room, almost colliding in the doorway with the Doctor and Mike Yates who were just arriving.

'I see you're in your usual sweet, affable mood, Brigadier,' said the Doctor.

Mike Yates gave an involuntary grin – and straightened his face just too late.

'When you've quite finished grinning like a Cheshire cat, Captain Yates,' said the Brigadier icily, 'perhaps you would continue with your duties?'

'Sir!' Mike Yates snapped to attention, threw up a hurried salute, and left the Brigadier's office even more rapidly than Benton.

Quite unintimidated, the Doctor looked down at the Brigadier.

41

'Now then, Brigadier, in a moment you can tell me what all the fuss is about. But first . . .'

On the other side of the square from UNIT HQ a Telephone Company workman was working on a big junction box that stood on the pavement, attaching a small but complex circuit into the maze of wiring inside.

His task completed, the workman took a little black box from his pocket, extended its aerial, checked its functioning, then closed the aerial and returned the device to his pocket . . .

In the UNIT main office, Mike Yates took his ear from the receiver. 'Still there, Mr Carr? Oh, good. For a moment I thought we'd been cut off . . .'

The workman closed the junction box and went into the nearby canvas hut, which contained a rickety table and chair, kettle and tea-making equipment and not much else.

Taking the device from his pocket he stood it on the table, and extended the aerial again and switched on.

Mike Yates's voice could be heard, a little tinny, but perfectly clear. 'As I was saying, the escort will be under my command, and will consist of my Sergeant and four motor-cycle outriders.'

'Bit light isn't it?' grumbled a second voice. 'Considering the importance of this weapon – '

Yates's voice concluded the sentence ' – we'll only make ourselves more conspicuous if we surround it with a small army, won't we?'

'All right, I suppose you people know best.'

'Our rendezvous with you will be at 0815 hours.'

'You'll let me know the projected route?'

'I'll ring it through as soon as its finalised. Goodbye, Mr Carr.'

'Goodbye.' A click, and then silence.

While all this was going on, an extraordinary scene took place in the little hut.

The listener removed his cap and muffler. He took off his grimy coveralls to reveal an immaculately cut Savile Row suit, a spotless white handkerchief in the top pocket. Finally he slipped his hands under his chin and removed his face, peeling back the mask of the workman to reveal a very different set of features.

The face beneath the mask, although rather sallow, was distinguished in a somewhat sinister way, with heavy eyebrows, dark, burning eyes, and a neatly pointed beard.

It was the face of the Master.

A renegade Time Lord, dedicated to evil for evil's sake, and the Doctor's oldest and bitterest enemy.

The transformation complete, the Master took a fur-collared overcoat from the back of a chair, tossed it carelessly over one arm, and strolled out of the canvas hut, every inch the man of distinction.

Parked not far away was a luxury limousine, with a chauffeur as big and black and powerful as the car he drove.

As the Master appeared, the chauffeur sprang from the car, touched his cap and opened the rear door.

The Master slid gracefully into the back seat, sank back into the expensive leather upholstery, and produced and lit a large and opulent cigar.

Exhaling a cloud of fragrant smoke, he produced the listening device and settled back to wait.

The Doctor had refused even to discuss the problems of the Peace Conference until the Brigadier had heard and agreed to his own demands concerning Stangmoor Prison.

'All right,' said the Brigadier at last. 'All right, all right, Doctor. You win!'

The Doctor was taking no chances. 'You'll back my report to the Home Office calling for a complete ban on the Keller Process?'

'Yes.'

'And you'll chase up the Home Secretary to see he takes some action?'

'*Yes*, Doctor! And if that doesn't do any good, I personally will go down to Stangmoor and blow the wretched machine up. Now, are you or are you not, going to help me with this case?'

The Doctor beamed at him. 'My dear Lethbridge-Stewart, your wish is my command. If there's anything I can do to help, you know you have only to ask!'

'Thank you,' said the Brigadier through gritted teeth, and jumped to his feet. Snatching up his cap and swagger stick, he headed for the door.

'Where on Earth do you think you're going?'

'To see the new Chinese Delegate – Fu Peng.'

'Fu Peng?' said the Doctor thoughtfully. 'He must be Hokkien.'

The Brigadier paused in the doorway. 'No, no, Doctor, he's Chinese! Come along!'

With the Doctor close behind, the Brigadier marched through the outer office. As he passed, Mike Yates rose to his feet and held out a sheaf of papers. 'Sir – '

'Later,' snapped the Brigadier, and passed by without breaking his stride.

The Doctor paused, giving Mike a sympathetic smile. 'I can see it's going to be one of those days!'

Mike grinned, and the Doctor said reprovingly, 'Cheshire cat, Cheshire cat, Captain Yates!' He followed the Brigadier out of the office.

Mike Yates sat down again, and picked up the phone. 'Get me transport will you?'

The Master sat at his ease in the back of his limousine, puffing luxuriously at his cigar. The little black box with the aerial lay on the seat beside him, and from it came Mike Yates's voice. 'Transport? Captain Yates here. I'd like you to lay on a four-man motor cycle escort and a jeep for 0700 hours. I'll be taking the party down myself.'

'Righto, sir.'

Again, there was a click and then silence.

Suddenly the Master leaned forward, staring intently out of the window.

Two men were coming down the steps of the big house on the side of the square. One was a tall man in Army Officer's uniform. The second, even taller, wore a flowing cape, and had a shock of untidy white hair.

The Master stroked his beard, his lips drawing back in a smile that was very like a snarl.

The Doctor! His ancient enemy, trapped as he was himself on this miserable planet. Trapped, and soon like the planet itself, due to be destroyed by the Master's vengeance.

5

The Pistol

Despite his high rank, the new Chinese Delegate wore the simple collarless tunic made popular at that time by China's revered leader, Mao Tse-Tung.

He sat at his desk, stern-featured and scowling, studying papers, refusing even to look up as the Brigadier and the Doctor were shown in to his suite.

Standing before the desk, the Brigadier extended his hand. 'Mr Fu Peng? I am Brigadier Lethbridge-Stewart of UNIT Command. I'm in charge of all security arrangements.'

Fu Peng ignored the outstretched hand.

Restraining his annoyance, the Brigadier went on. 'And this is the Doctor, our Scientific Adviser.'

The Doctor stepped forward, bowed, and produced a string of melodious syllables. To the astonished Brigadier they began something like. 'Wah-pye chiah lu-lai . . .'

He lost track of the rest.

Immediately Fu Peng looked up, an astonished smile spreading over his heavy features. The Doctor was speaking fluent Chinese, and not only Chinese but the Hokkien dialect of Fu Peng's native province.

(What the Doctor had actually said was, 'This humble and unworthy person welcomes you, and delights in your safe arrival.')

Fu Peng rose, bowed in return and spoke in the same

language. 'Thank you for your courtesy and for your welcome. It is I who am delighted to meet such a charming person in this barbaric land.' For the sake of courtesy, Fu Peng continued in English. 'It is rare to meet a Westerner who knows our language.'

'Thank you,' said the Doctor modestly. 'I fear that my Hokkien is somewhat rusty.'

'On the contrary, it is excellent.' Fu Peng clicked his fingers, and an aide scurried from the room. 'Please be seated.'

The Doctor sat. 'Well, it's many years since I had a chance to speak Hokkien. The last time, I remember was a conversation with Tse-Tung. It was on the Long March, I remember and . . .'

Fu Peng gave him an astonished look. 'Tse-Tung! That is the personal name of our Chairman, Mao Tse-Tung.'

The Doctor nodded and said casually. 'He himself gave me leave to use it.'

Deeply impressed, Fu Peng bowed again.

The Brigadier had been standing there ignored all this time. 'Well, gentlemen,' he said hopefully. 'If we could just discuss the immediate problem?'

No one took any notice.

Fu Peng's aide came back into the room, carrying a heavy tray which bore all the requisites for the ceremonial serving of Chinese tea.

Fu Peng turned to the Doctor. 'You will take tea with me?'

The Doctor rose, bowed, and said something that sounded like, 'Kum-Siah.'

Fu Peng snapped an order to the aide, who carried the tray over to a table by the window.

Fu Peng waved the Doctor to a seat. 'You have heard of the great tragedy that has befallen my country-man?'

47

'Yes, indeed. I am here to do all I can to help.'

Fu Peng sat down himself and began pouring tea. 'It is a great sadness . . .'

Since by now the Doctor and Fu Peng had slipped back into Hokkien Chinese, the Brigadier listened to the exchange in total bafflement.

The Doctor and Fu Peng went on talking in low earnest voices. Ignored, the Brigadier sank into a chair and sat down to wait.

Escorted by Prison Officer Green, Lenny Vosper trudged down the prison corridors with his bucket and mop. Vosper was a dangerous thug with a record of violence. By careful good behaviour he had managed to become a 'Trusty', a long term prisoner allowed certain privileges because he was reckoned to be at least partly reformed. Vosper was uneasily aware of the tension in the prison, of the angry murmuring coming from the cells they passed. Moreover, Vosper had his own reasons for feeling tense.

Green marched him along the short corridor that led to the condemned cell and unlocked the door. 'All right, Vosper, get busy!'

Vosper shuffled into the cell and began mopping the floor.

From the main area of the prison came the angry muttering of the prisoners.

In the locked Process Chamber the Keller Machine was throbbing gently.

Jo Grant was in the Prison Infirmary visiting Barnham, the prisoner she had seen undergoing the Keller process.

The big man was laying contentedly back against his pillows, listening to the radio on headphones.

Jo looked at Doctor Summers. 'How is he?'

'Fit as a fiddle, aren't you Barnham?' He raised his voice. 'Barnham – a visitor for you.'

Realising he was being spoken to, Barnham slipped off the headphones, and looked up at Jo curiously. 'Hallo.'

Sitting in the chair beside the bed, Jo handed him a box of chocolates. 'Here, these are for you.'

Barnham gave her a child-like smile. 'Thank you. Do I know you, miss?'

'Well, we have sort of met.'

'It's just that I don't seem to remember anything much.'

'You were treated by the Keller Process. Don't you remember that?'

He shook his head. 'Everything seems a bit of a blank,' he said in a slow, puzzled voice. 'You won't believe this, but I couldn't even remember my own name till the doctor here told me who I was.'

There was something about his blank, child-like expression that made Jo suddenly uneasy. She stood up. 'Well, I'm glad to see you looking so much better. Goodbye.'

'Bye bye, miss, and thank you for the chocolates.' Barnham spoke like a well-mannered child in junior school. He put back the headphones and leaned back, closing his eyes.

Jo moved over to Doctor Summers. 'Well, everything seems to be all right.'

'I'm not so sure,' said Summers worriedly. 'My theory is that in Barnham's case the Machine over-reacted. It extracted *all* the negative impulses from his brain.'

Jo looked at the peaceful figure in the bed. 'So what does that make him now?'

Summers shrugged. 'Depends how you look at it. An idiot – or a saint?'

* * *

The noise from down the corridor was getting louder now.

Vosper said casually, 'Getting a bit noisy out there, aren't they, Mr Green?'

Green turned and shouted down the corridor. 'All right, you lot, shut up, can't you?'

In a flash, Vosper took a plastic-wrapped bundle from the bottom of his bucket of water, and thrust it under the mattress on the already made-up bed. When Green came back into the cell, Vosper was vigorously mopping the last section of floor.

'Finish up,' said Green. 'Here they come.'

He looked along the corridor as a little group of people came marching towards the cell. One was a prisoner, flanked by two prison officers. Behind came the Governor, and Chief Prison Officer Powers.

Green stood aside as the little group entered the cell. 'All right, Vosper, outside.'

Snatching up his bucket and mop, Vosper made for the door, catching the new prisoner's eye for a moment as he scurried away.

The new prisoner, Mailer, was a tough hard-bitten character with brutal features. His face had a weathered, corrugated look, as if made of leather rather than normal skin.

Harry Mailer was a London gang leader, a vicious killer who had run a highly successful protection racket with the aid of a gang of armed thugs. He had finally been arrested and convicted for a murder which he had been rash enough to commit more or less in public. It was thought to be only one of a whole string of murders in which no evidence, and indeed no bodies, had ever been found. It was rumoured that Mailer's victims were embedded in the foundations of bridges and motorways all over England.

Like many criminals of his type, Mailer was both

arrogant and conceited. He looked disparagingly around the well-furnished cell. 'Proper little home from home, isn't it?'

The Governor said, 'You'll be in this cell until sentence is carried out, Mailer.'

Coolly Mailer stretched out on the bed. 'I wouldn't put any money on that, Governor. Nobody's going to turn me into a ruddy zombie – and that includes you, mate.'

Chief Prison Officer Powers was outraged. 'That's enough of that, Mailer – '

The Governor smiled grimly, prepared to allow Mailer his gesture of defiance. 'All right, Chief.' He left the cell.

Powers glared angrily down at Mailer for a moment, then turned to the two warders who had brought him. 'Watch him!'

Powers and Green too left the cell. With a clang of metal and a rattle of keys, the door was closed and locked behind them.

The warders were Johnson and Samuels, the same two kindly, middle-aged men who had looked after Barnham. Johnson nodded towards the pack of cards on the table. 'Care for a game, Harry? It'll pass the time.'

'Drop dead,' said Mailer briefly.

The warder shrugged. 'Suit yourself. Sam?'

The two warders sat down. One of them shuffled the cards and they began to play, comfortable in their long-established routine.

Harry Mailer watched them for a moment, then slipped a hand under the mattress. His fingers encountered a hard, nobbly bundle, cold metal under wet plastic.

Quickly Mailer withdrew his hand. Next time the warders glanced at him he was laying back, eyes closed, a picture of innocent relaxation.

* * *

51

To the Brigadier's relief the tea party between the Doctor and Fu Peng seemed to be drawing to a close. Still chatting away in Chinese, they rose and bowed ceremonially to each other.

The Brigadier leaped to his feet. 'There are a few questions I should like Mr Fu Peng . . .'

Another burst of Chinese.

The Brigadier looked at the Doctor. 'What did he say?'

'Dried squid and stewed jellyfish.'

The Brigadier blinked, wondering if this was some obscure Chinese insult. 'What?'

'For our dinner,' explained the Doctor. 'He's invited me to dine.' He bowed once again to Fu Peng, and said in Hokkien, 'Farewell, my dear Peng.'

Fu Peng bowed in return. 'Until our next meeting, Doctor.'

The Brigadier made a last desperate attempt to get someone to take some notice of him. 'I really must insist on asking – '

But Fu Peng had returned to the study of his papers, and the Doctor was already at the door.

'Do hurry along, old chap. We've got a lot of work to do!'

Fuming, the Brigadier followed him from the suite.

Pouring himself a large brandy from the bar in the back of his limousine, the Master was still listening to Mike Yates's voice. 'Armoury? Captain Yates here. I want to draw arms and ammunition for a minimum escort detail, Security Coding 27953/4A/22 . . .'

The Master sat back listening, sipping his brandy.

Moving cautiously, inch by inch, Mailer slid the gun from the plastic bag beneath the mattress.

When the butt was in his hand he lay patiently

waiting. At last he heard footsteps and the rattle of crockery from the corridor.

Suddenly he spoke. 'Where's the food then – or are you planning to starve me to death?'

Johnson looked up. 'It's coming, Mailer, it's coming.'

'So's Christmas!'

There was the sound of a key in the lock and the cell door began to open.

'About time,' grunted Mailer.

The warder with the tray came into the cell, and with sudden, shocking speed, Mailer sprang from the bed, grabbing the man from behind and jamming the pistol against his ear. The tray crashed to the floor.

Mailer glared at the other two warders. 'You two, stay right where you are, or he gets it right now.'

The two warders stood very still.

Mailer jabbed his captive with the barrel of the automatic. '*You!* Give me the keys.' Frozen with fear the man didn't move.

Mailer jabbed him again. 'I said the keys. Hand 'em over. Move!'

6

The Dragon

The Brigadier sat at his desk, struggling to absorb the astonishing theory that had just been presented to him. 'A connection? Between what happened at Stangmoor, and what's been happening at the Conference?'

The Doctor was staring abstractedly out of the window. 'Another mysterious corpse with an expression of terror? There's got to be a connection.'

The Brigadier said, 'But this Keller Machine of yours is miles away.'

The Doctor nodded. 'The power must be – relayed in some way . . .'

He fell silent, lost in thought.

Mike Yates bustled in. 'Excuse me sir, we're just about ready for off. If you'd okay the movement order and the route plans?'

He handed the Brigadier a sheaf of papers.

The Brigadier leafed through them, initialling each page.

'Off on a little jaunt, Captain Yates?' asked the Doctor.

'We're moving the Thunderbolt – a nuclear powered missile with a war-head full of nerve gas. Not exactly a jaunt, Doctor.'

'I thought those things had been outlawed?'

'They have. This one's on the way to the Naval dockyard. The Navy are going to dump it in the depths of the ocean.'

'With the Peace Conference going on? Not a very tactful time to be trundling rockets about, is it?'

The Brigadier looked up from the papers. 'I see you're taking Sergeant Benton?'

'If it's okay with you, sir.'

'You're welcome to him. Just be sure he doesn't lose the missile for you. He managed to lose a Chinese girl in broad daylight!'

The Doctor looked up. 'Chinese girl? What Chinese girl?'

The Brigadier handed back the papers. 'All right, Yates. Carry on, and good luck!'

Mike Yates saluted. 'Thank you, sir. Bye Doctor!' He hurried from the room.

'Brigadier!' thundered the Doctor. '*What Chinese girl?*'

'Captain Chin Lee, the late General's aide. I thought she might be implicated, so I had her followed. Benton lost her.'

The Doctor jumped up. 'That's it. That's the connection. When Emil Keller installed the Machine at Stangmoor, he had a Chinese girl as his assistant.'

'Could be coincidence.'

'Coincidence, my foot. You'd better put out a general alert for that Chinese girl, Brigadier. Wherever she is, she's got to be found!'

In fact, Captain Chin Lee wasn't very far away. She was walking towards the Master's limousine, which was parked in a nearby back street.

The Master opened the door and patted the seat beside him. 'You are late, Chin Lee.'

Chin Lee entered the car. 'My apologies, Master.'

'You did well at the Conference. Now I have another task for you.'

Chin Lee shrank back, her eyes widening in fear. 'No. Please, no . . .'

The Master's hand shot out, seizing her neck like a clamp, his fingers adjusting the little metal disc behind her ear. His voice was deep, soothing, hypnotic. 'You will obey my command, Chin Lee.'

'Yes, Master.'

'Tonight you will kill the American Delegate.'

Tonelessly Chin Lee repeated, 'I will kill the American Delegate . . .'

'Good,' said the Master gently. 'Now go – and obey me.'

Chin Lee got out of the car and moved away

Harry Mailer had laid his plans well. Very soon the Special Wing was under his control. The three prison officers were lined up in the corridor, guarded by Mailer and half-a-dozen released prisoners.

Among the captives was Prison Officer Green, still quite unintimidated. 'You'll never get away with this, Mailer,' he growled. 'You've got no chance.'

Mailer gestured threateningly with the pistol. 'Shut up. One more peep out of you – '

He was interrupted by the arrival of Vosper. 'I've fixed the phones Harry, but they've got the Wing surrounded.'

From outside there came the wail of an alarm siren. 'They won't bust in,' said Mailer confidently. 'Not while we've got some of their screws here.'

'Oh, sure,' said Vosper gloomily. 'They can't get in – but we can't get out.'

'We'll get out,' snarled Mailer. 'Shut up and let me think.'

'We can't just stay here, Harry. They'll starve us out.'

'We need hostages.'

Vosper nodded towards the three prison officers. 'We've got these.'

'We need more. If we cut round behind the kitchens,

we can get to the Hospital, maybe grab ourselves a doctor.' He turned to one of the prisoners. 'You and the others stay here. Lenny, you come with me.'

They hurried out.

When the alarms started going off, Jo Grant had gone to the telephone in an attempt to find out what was going on. A panicky prison officer had begun giving her a confused account of a breakout in the Special Wing and had suddenly been cut off.

Jo rattled the receiver. 'It's no good, the phone's still dead.'

'I think you'd better make for the Administration Block, Miss Grant.'

'What about you?'

'I'd better stay here. Someone's bound to get hurt before all this is over . . .'

Suddenly the door was flung open. Two prisoners were standing there – one of them had a pistol in his hand.

At a nod from Mailer, Vosper grabbed Summers in a painful arm lock and shoved him out of the room.

With the barrel of the automatic, Mailer motioned Jo towards the door. 'Out! Come on, on your way!'

Reluctantly Jo obeyed.

The Doctor too was having some trouble with the telephone.

'Operator, I've been waiting some time for my call to Stangmoor Prison . . . I see. Yes, very well, I'll hold.' He looked up at the Brigadier. 'Some trouble with the lines, apparently.'

Before the Brigadier could reply, the phone on his desk rang. He lifted the receiver. 'Lethbridge-Stewart. What? Where? No, don't arrest her. I'll deal with this myself.' He put down the phone and turned to the Doctor. 'Chin

Lee's turned up again. She's just been seen entering the Chinese Delegate's suite. Thing is, the place is deserted. Apparently your friend Fu Peng is out at some Embassy reception.' The Brigadier reached for his hat. 'Come along, Doctor, you can call Miss Grant later . . .'

The Chinese Delegate's suite was silent and empty as Chin Lee came into the room.

She stood in the doorway for a moment, a hand to her temples, her mind filled with a strange electronic pulsing sound.

Then, her face calm and distant, she went over to the telephone. 'Room 411 please . . . Hello, is the American Delegate there? This is Captain Chin Lee of the Chinese People's Delegation. I must speak to Senator Alcott urgently . . .'

Senator Alcott, the American Delegate was a distinguished looking man in his sixties with a tanned face and snowy white hair. He had passed up the Reception for a working dinner in his suite, and he was considerably astonished when his aide told him of Chin Lee's call.

Wiping his mouth with his napkin, he went into the adjoining office and picked up the phone. 'Alcott here.'

'This is Captain Chin Lee.'

'Yes, Captain. What can I do for you?'

'Comrade Fu Peng wishes to speak to you immediately. He wonders if you could come to our suite.'

'At this time of night?'

'It is a matter of vital importance. He wishes to assure you that the meeting will be to your country's advantage.'

Alcott played for time. 'This is highly irregular . . .'

'He asks that you come alone. The subject is most secret.'

Alcott considered. So, the Chinese were anxious to make some kind of secret deal. You couldn't trust them, of course – but at least he ought to listen. 'Okay, Captain, I'll be right over . . .'

'Your time will not be wasted, Senator,' said Chin Lee. She put down the phone, and went out into the little hallway of the suite. She unlocked the door, left it a little ajar, concealed herself in an alcove and waited.

Minutes later, there came a tap on the door. An American voice called, 'Anyone home? Mr Fu Peng? Are you there?'

Alcott came cautiously into the little hall.

He looked around, saw the open door to the main suite. 'Mr Fu Peng, are you there?'

He went over to the suite and went inside.

Chin Lee crossed the hall, followed him into the suite and closed the door behind her.

Surprised, Alcott swung round. 'May I ask what this is about, Captain? Where is Mr Fu Peng?'

'He will be here soon, Senator. Please, sit down.'

'Now look, I'm right in the middle of dinner – '

'Please, sit down Senator Alcott.' The voice was strangely commanding.

'All right, but let's make it short, shall we?' Sulkily, Alcott sat down.

Chin Lee went to the switch and turned off the lights. Immediately suspicious, Alcott leaped to his feet again. 'Hey, what are you doing?'

A strange electronic throbbing was filling the room.

Alcott shook his head to clear it. 'I can hear this noise . . .' He clawed at his collar. 'Why is it so hot in here? Hey, what's happening?'

Senator Alcott had been fighting Communism all his life, particularly the Chinese variety. Intellectually, he knew that somehow America and China must co-operate, but in his heart he still distrusted the Chinese – and feared them, too.

He stared hard at the impassive, motionless figure of Chin Lee. Suddenly her body seemed to shimmer, to distort and change. All at once, instead of the small figure of the Chinese girl, Alcott saw a great Chinese dragon, the terrifying embodiment of all his fears.

He stared in horror at the great teeth, the scaly body and the great bulging eyes, and the fearsome claws.

'Get back,' he screamed.

The monster reared up to destroy him.

7

The Hostage

The door to the suite was flung open, revealing the Doctor, the Brigadier and Fu Peng on the threshold.

So powerful was the force from Chin Lee's mind that all three saw the looming monster just as clearly as did Alcott himself.

The Brigadier drew his revolver and took aim.

'No, Brigadier, don't!' shouted the Doctor.

As the Brigadier fired, the Doctor knocked his arm up, and the shot went wild.

The Doctor advanced steadily on the dragon. It wasn't real – he knew it couldn't be real – but it took every atom of his will to conquer the illusion.

Suddenly the dragon began to blur, to become transparent . . .

Straining his eyes, the Brigadier saw the form of Chin Lee standing behind it. He heard the Doctor shout something in Chinese, saw him leap forward and flick his hand lightly at Chin Lee's neck.

Chin Lee collapsed – and the dragon disappeared. The Doctor caught her as she fell and lowered her gently to the ground.

Fu Peng said softly, 'That was one of the legendary dragon-demons of my people.'

'A collective hallucination, gentlemen,' said the Doctor briskly. He knelt beside the body of Alcott. 'Who's this?'

'It's the American Delegate!' said the Brigadier appalled. 'Is he dead?'

'No, but he's suffering from acute shock.'

Chin Lee's hair was disarranged and Fu Peng spotted the metal disc gleaming on her neck. 'What is this, Doctor?'

Gently the Doctor removed it. 'A telepathic amplifier!'

The Brigadier looked puzzled. 'Is that what caused the hallucinations?'

'Not caused them,' said the Doctor slowly. 'It picked up the impulses and projected them through Chin Lee's mind.'

'Picked them up from where?'

'Unless I'm very much mistaken, from the Keller Machine at Stangmoor Prison.'

Doctor Summers was still protesting as they were pushed along the corridor to the Special Wing by a couple of the freed prisoners. 'Can't you at least let me stay in the infirmary? I've got a patient there, Barnham. He's in a critical condition.'

'Shut up,' snarled Mailer.

Vosper said worriedly. 'The whole wing's surrounded, Harry. There's hundreds of them.'

'All right, I know.'

'Show some sense, Mailer,' said Doctor Summers. 'You'll never get away with it.'

'They could rush us any minute,' said Vosper.

'They won't while we've got these,' said Mailer confidently. 'Vosper, you get busy and fix those phones again. I want to talk to the Governor.'

Vosper nodded. 'What about these two? What are you going to do with them?'

'Put 'em in the guest room.'

Mailer shoved Jo and Doctor Summers into the condemned cell.

'You'll never get away with it,' said Summers again.

'Shut up,' said Mailer. 'Go on, get moving. Chuck them inside, you two!'

Taking Mailer at his word, the prisoners threw first Summers then Jo into the condemned cell. Mailer slammed and locked the door behind them.

Jo stumbled and fell across the bed. Summers picked himself up, went across and helped her to rise. 'Are you all right?'

She winced. 'Yes, more or less.'

'Come and sit down.' They both sat on the bed.

Jo rubbed her bruises. 'Now what?'

Summers sighed. 'I wish I knew!'

Senator Alcott had been carried off in an ambulance. Watched by Fu Peng and the Brigadier, the Doctor was examining Chin Lee, who had been lifted on to a sofa.

She moaned and stirred.

'This girl has done great harm,' said Fu Peng severely. 'She must be punished.'

'She wasn't really responsible, you know,' said the Doctor mildly.

'Doctor, I have understood very little of what you have been saying. Please explain more clearly.'

'Well, briefly, Chin Lee was being *used* – by someone who wants to drive the world into war.'

'You will find this person and punish him?'

'If I can, Fu Peng.'

Fu Peng said gravely. 'Then I will leave matters to you. Now I must go to my Embassy. May the gods smile on you, Doctor.'

He bowed, the Doctor bowed in return, and Fu Peng left the suite.

The Doctor leaned over Chin Lee. 'Can you hear me? Chin Lee! Can you hear me? Listen to me.'

Chin Lee muttered something in Chinese.

The Doctor cocked his head. 'Ah, Cantonese!' In the same Chinese dialect he said, 'Trust me, Chin Lee. Trust me.'

Next time Chin Lee spoke it was in English. 'Something happened,' she said dazedly. 'Something terrible.'

'It was in your mind,' said the Doctor gently. 'Only in your mind. Now I must ask you some questions, Chin Lee. About Emil Keller . . . and your visit to Stangmoor Prison.'

'Well,' demanded Mailer. 'Did you fix the phones?'

Vosper shook his head. 'Sorry, Harry, no luck. I fixed 'em too good in the first place!'

'Charming! How are we going to do a deal with the Governor if we can't talk to him?' Mailer considered, then tossed Vosper the keys. 'All right, get that door open.'

Vosper opened the door to the condemned cell.

Immediately Summers jumped to his feet and rushed at Vosper, who dodged.

Mailer stepped quickly forwards and knocked Summers down with his pistol. He laughed. 'All right, Doc, on your feet. You're getting out of here.'

Jo helped Summers to get up. 'Seen some sense at last have you?' She tried to leave the cell, but Mailer shoved her back.

'Not you, darling.' He grabbed Summers by the arm. 'As for you, mate, you're taking a message to the Governor.'

'What message?' said Summers feebly.

'I want a safe conduct out of here for me and everyone in the Special Wing.'

'I'm not leaving without Miss Grant.'

'Oh, yes you are, mate!' said Mailer, and dragged him away.

'Don't worry,' called Jo. 'I'll be all right.'

Mailer shoved Summers towards Vosper. 'All right, get him moving.' He turned back to Jo. 'If I were you, I'd get some sleep.' With that, the cell door was slammed shut once again.

Head pillowed on his arms, the Brigadier was dozing at his desk, dreaming of his days as a subaltern, and a young lady called Doris.

He jerked awake as the Doctor strode into the room and drew the curtains. 'Rise and shine, Brigadier, I've brought someone to see you.'

Rubbing his eyes, the Brigadier saw Chin Lee standing beside the Doctor. 'Good morning, Captain. Won't you sit down?'

'Thank you,' said Chin Lee. Like the Doctor, she looked appallingly fresh and wide awake.

The Brigadier flicked the intercom. 'Corporal Bell. Organise some coffee, will you?'

'Right away, sir.'

'Now then, Brigadier,' said the Doctor briskly. 'I've had a good long talk with Chin Lee. I think you'll find she can cast quite a bit of light on what's been happening.'

'I'm glad to hear that someone can, Doctor!'

'Well, now, Chin Lee,' said the Doctor. 'Let's start – '

The telephone rang and the Brigadier picked it up. 'Oh, it's you, Yates. How are you getting on?' The Brigadier listened. 'Oh, I see. Hold on.' He turned to the Doctor. 'It's Yates. He's had a bit of a hold-up with his – er – cargo. Trouble with a crane.'

The Doctor looked puzzled.

The Brigadier looked meaningly at Chin Lee, not wanting to be more explicit.

The Doctor followed his glance and grinned. 'Oh, I see. Well, tell him to be careful with his – er – cargo!'

The Brigadier gave him a quelling look, and returned to the telephone. 'What's that, Yates? Yes, she's here now. There's been quite a bit of trouble here too . . .'

The Master sat back in his limousine, listening to the voices on the UNIT phone.

He heard Mike Yates's voice ask, 'Really, sir? What happened?'

'Well, as far as I can make out, she tried to scare the American Delegate to death with a hallucination, but the Doctor stopped her.'

The Master leaned forwards, frowning.

Yates said, 'Don't think I quite follow, sir.'

'Quite frankly, Captain Yates, neither do I. Apparently it's all to do with the Keller Machine at Stangmoor prison.'

The Master flicked off the listening device. After a moment, he smiled to himself. It never did to underestimate the Doctor. Who would have thought he would have reached the truth so quickly?

The Master slid back the partition that divided him from his chauffeur. 'Stangmoor Prison, if you please.'

The limousine swept smoothly away.

The Brigadier was interrogating Chin Lee. This time she answered his questions without hesitation. It had taken the Doctor most of the night to loosen the Master's hypnotic grip on her mind, but now she was more or less herself again, and at least willing to tell what she could.

'Where did you first meet this Emil Keller?'

'At an Embassy reception, Brigadier. He talked to me about the Keller Process for reforming the habitual criminal. He invited me to visit Stangmoor Prison with him.'

'You agreed to go? May I ask why?'

With a hint of her old severity, Chin Lee said, 'Prison

reform is high on our list of priorities in Peking, Brigadier.'

'Can you tell us what happened at Stangmoor?'

'I know that we went to the Process Chamber. But I can't remember . . .' Her voice tailed away.

'Did you see this man Keller again?'

'Yes, many times I think. But if I try to think about it, my mind becomes confused . . .'

'Post-hypnotic block,' explained the Doctor. 'His usual technique.'

'Whose usual technique?'

'Think, man,' urged the Doctor. 'Who else would make a deliberate attempt to plunge the world into war – using techniques and equipment not even developed on Earth?' The Doctor held out his hand, the telepathic amplifier in his palm.

The Brigadier gave him a horrified look. 'The Master?'

The Doctor nodded. 'The Master – otherwise known as Emil Keller.'

Once released, Doctor Summers had made for the Governor's office, a comfortable old-fashioned room, ornamented with shields, regimental photographs, and a suit of armour. He leaned forwards over the Governor's desk. 'Please, listen to me, Governor. You've *got* to negotiate.'

'I'm sorry, Doctor Summers, that's out of the question.'

'But you're risking innocent lives!'

'Suppose I do turn Mailer loose? And those other thugs with him? They'd kill anyone who got in their way. How many innocent lives would I be risking then?'

Summers was silent, realising the truth of what the Governor had said.

Chief Prison Officer Powers said, 'We've done everything we can, Doctor Summers. The Special Wing is sealed off. If they get the slightest chance, my men will rush the block.'

'And if they don't get a chance?'

'We'll wait it out,' said the Governor. 'Mailer's not stupid, he knows he can't hold out for ever. Once he realises he can't bluff me – '

'But Mailer isn't bluffing,' said Summers desperately. 'He's a killer – and he means what he says. What about Miss Grant?'

'Miss Grant is a member of UNIT,' said the Governor stolidly. 'She is here on duty, like the rest of us.' He looked sympathetically at Summers's anguished face. 'All I can do is inform her headquarters of the situation.'

Finally, even the Brigadier had run out of questions. He sent off Chin Lee under the charge of Corporal Bell and turned to the Doctor. 'Well, what am I to do with her?'

'Let her go, of course, she's not a criminal. She won't do any more harm, now I've got the telepathic amplifier.'

The telephone rang and the Brigadier lifted the receiver. 'Yes?' He listened for some minutes, then turned worriedly to the Doctor. 'There's trouble at Stang Moor.'

'Is Jo all right? Well?' snapped the Doctor.

For a moment the Brigadier didn't reply.

'Miss Grant's been captured, Doctor. She's being held as a hostage.'

By now Jo Grant had been taken from her cell. She was standing with Vosper and Mailer and the other hostages just inside the door that led from the Special Block to the rest of the prison.

Mailer was shouting to the warders on the other side of the door. 'Do you hear me out there? This is your last chance. Either we walk out of here, or this lot gets it – and the girl goes first.' He raised his revolver and held it to Jo's head. 'So come on, Governor – what are you going to do about it?'

8

The Mutiny

After a quick visit to the besieged Special Wing, Chief Prison Officer Powers returned to the Governor's office looking very worried. 'The prisoners are getting very nasty, sir. Threatening to shoot Miss Grant and the other hostages.'

Doctor Summers turned to the Governor. 'Please, you must talk to them.'

The Governor hesitated for a moment. 'All right. At the moment it's a deadlock. Maybe I can make Mailer see sense.'

Mailer jabbed the muzzle of his automatic against Jo's neck. 'Time's running out for you, love.'

Jo looked fearlessly up at him. 'And for you!'

Vosper came hurrying from the gate. 'The Governor's on his way over, Harry.'

'Right. When he gets here, let him in.'

Vosper stared at him. 'In here?'

'Well, I'm not going out there, am I?' said Mailer reasonably. 'Anyway, he won't try anything.'

Vosper turned to another prisoner. 'You heard. When the Governor arrives, open the door and let him in. Just the Governor, mind.'

The prisoner hurried away.

Suddenly Vosper looked over Mailer's shoulder, his eyes widening. 'Harry, look!'

Mailer turned. A burly figure in hospital dressing gown and pyjamas was wandering down the steps.

'It's Barnham,' whispered Vosper. 'The bloke they put under the Keller Machine. He must have come over from the infirmary.'

Barnham smiled pathetically at them, rather like a lost child. 'I'm looking for Doctor Summers,' he said softly. 'Has anyone seen Doctor Summers?'

Mailer shuddered. This was the fate that had been intended for him. 'Get him out of here, he gives me the creeps.'

Vosper tapped one of the other prisoners on the shoulder. 'Come on, you, give me a hand.'

Mailer was staring at Barnham in fascinated horror – and Jo seized her chance. Leaping forward, she grabbed hold of the big automatic, trying desperately to wrench it from Mailer's hand.

Mailer's finger tightened on the trigger, the gun fired – and one of the prisoners fell dead.

The shock of the unexpected explosion made Mailer drop the gun. It slid across the floor and Jo dived after it. Before Mailer could react, Prison Officer Green jumped on him.

Free of the threat of Mailer's gun the two other guards attacked the nearest prisoners, and a general struggle broke out.

Jo snatched up the gun – and wondered what to do next. Barnham, who had been watching the fighting with uncomprehending terror cowered back against the wall, his face twisted as if he was going to cry. 'It's all right, Barnham, hide,' called Jo.

She fired a shot in the air, with a confused idea of summoning help. Strangely enough it worked. The shot distracted the prisoners who were admitting the Governor. Seizing the opportunity, Powers and his men barged their way through the door, driving the rebel prisoners back by sheer weight of numbers.

Green landed a lucky punch that sent Mailer sprawling at Jo's feet.

There were shouts, the pounding of feet and suddenly warders were flooding into the wing, grabbing the mutinous prisoners and dragging them away. Mailer scrambled to his feet – and found Jo covering him with his own gun.

Jo saw Doctor Summers, Powers and the Governor hurrying towards her. Proudly she waved at Mailer with the automatic. 'There you are, Governor – he's all yours!'

A black limousine swept up the drive towards Stangmoor Prison. After its occupant had produced all the necessary passes, it was allowed to drive along the outer ring-road and through into the inner courtyard.

A few minutes later, there was a tap on the Governor's door, and Powers entered. 'Professor Keller to see you, sir.'

The Governor rose. 'All right, Mr Powers. Ah, there you are, Professor!'

An elegant, bearded figure followed Powers into the room. 'A great pleasure to see you again, Governor.'

'I'm by no means sure I can return the compliment, Professor,' said the Governor rather dourly. He sat down and waved the Professor to a seat.

The Professor – or as he was more usually known, the Master – looked hurt. 'I'm sorry to hear that, Governor.' He put down his briefcase and slipped out of his fur-collared overcoat. Instinctively, Powers came forward to take it from him and hang it up. 'Thank you very much,' said the Master. 'Now then, Governor, what seems to be the trouble?'

72

'There's been nothing *but* trouble since that Machine of yours was installed.'

'There are bound to be one or two teething troubles, but I'll soon take care of them for you.'

Such was the warmth and charm of the Master's personality, that the Governor felt his problems were already solved. 'You really think you can get things back to normal?'

'I'm sure of it.'

'Well, I hope so. We've even had UNIT down here investigating.'

The Master raised an eyebrow. 'Oh, really?'

'Yes, their Scientific Adviser is on his way down here now.'

The Master smiled. 'There's no need to trouble him, I assure you.' He tapped the big square briefcase at his feet. 'As you can see, I've brought my own equipment.'

'Let me take you to the Process Chamber.'

As the Master rose, he said, 'One thing before we go. I gather that the man who led the riot is next in line for the Process?'

'That's right, Harry Mailer.'

'Then I'd like to see him first of all, if I may?'

'Yes, of course.'

There was something about Professor Keller, reflected the Governor, that made it impossible to refuse him anything . . .

Harry Mailer was washing his face at the basin in the corner when the door opened and the Governor, Chief Prison Officer Powers, and a bearded stranger came into the cell.

The Governor nodded to the two warders. 'All right, Johnson, Samuels, you can wait outside.'

Puzzled, the two warders left the cell. Powers followed,

saying warningly, 'We'll be right outside, Mailer, so just watch yourself.'

The Governor said, 'Let us know when you've finished with him, Professor Keller.'

The Governor, too, left the cell, and the door was closed, leaving Mailer alone with the bearded stranger.

'He said "Keller",' said Mailer slowly. 'You're the bloke who invented the Machine. Pushing your luck, aren't you?'

The bearded man seemed amused. 'Well, perhaps I am, a little.'

Mailer advanced menacingly. 'Well, you'd better watch it, mate.' He made a sudden grab for the newcomer, who reached out almost casually, caught his wrist with one hand, and forced him down across the bed. Mailer found himself quite helpless, unable to move a muscle. 'What the – '

Smiling, the bearded man released him. 'Shut up, Mailer,' he said pleasantly. 'I've come to help you. You want to get out of here, don't you?'

Sulkily Mailer rubbed his wrist. 'I already tried that.'

'Yes, I heard about that pathetic little attempt. Doomed to failure. No proper plan, no resources.'

As he spoke, the newcomer laid his briefcase on the bed and opened it. To his amazement, Mailer saw that the case held several grenades, automatic revolvers, and what looked like a number of gas masks.

'Let me introduce myself, Mailer,' said the newcomer briskly. 'I am the Master – and you and I are going to cause a great deal of havoc in this prison.'

'Just you and me alone?'

The Master smiled. 'Well, not entirely. We have a powerful ally.'

* * *

In the Process Chamber the Keller Machine began throbbing angrily, as if aware of the violence to come. Waves of terror began spreading through the prison.

Waiting rather uneasily outside the cell, the Governor and the others heard the now-familiar yelling and banging from the cells. 'They're starting up again, Mr Green,' said Powers wearily. 'See if you can quieten them will you?'

'They probably think we're going to process Mailer right away,' said the Governor. He turned to the two warders. 'You two stay here, ready to let the Professor out. Come along Mr Powers, let's see if we can calm them down.'

The Governor and Powers moved away. 'That'll do there!' shouted Powers. 'Quieten down, will you, nothing's happening . . .'

In the cell the Master was completing Mailer's briefing. 'You'll find more arms and ammunition in the boot of my car. Don't forget, Mailer, you're responsible for taking over the main gate. Outwardly, I want this prison to appear to be running normally. I'm expecting a visitor, you see. Now, are you ready? You understand what to do?'

Mailer nodded. 'Got it.'

The Master rapped on the cell door and called. 'Right, I'm ready to come out now.'

The warder opened the door. To his astonishment he found himself facing two grotesquely masked figures. One of them threw something at his feet, there was a plop and a hiss, a cloud of smoke – and the warder knew no more. Mailer and the Master dashed from the cell. Another gas-grenade exploded at the feet of the second guard, who fell without a sound. As Mailer ran along the corridor, he saw the Governor descending the stairs.

Immediately, Mailer raised his automatic, and shot him down. Chief Officer Powers was close behind the Governor. Seeing what had happened, he turned and ran for the alarm just along the corridor. As his fingers touched the alarm, Mailer shot him in the back . . .

This time the prison break went according to plan – the Master's plan. Vosper and the rest of Mailer's cronies were released and armed. Warders were shot down and gassed as soon as they were encountered. The revolt spread with amazing speed. A party of prisoners broke out into the yard, secured yet more arms from the Master's car, and began distributing them throughout the prison.

Prisoners were released and armed, and they in turn released and armed more prisoners. In a surprisingly short space of time, the whole prison had been taken over.

As the fighting died down, the Master stood at the top of the steps leading to the main prison area and raised his voice. 'The rest of you, stay where you are until the gas clears. Get down on the floor. Don't worry, you'll all be released in time. The prison is in our hands!'

He ran to a nearby wall phone, ripped out the lead and began attaching a complex electronic device . . .

In the prison infirmary, Jo and Doctor Summers had just finished settling Barnham back into his bed.

When the alarm sounded, they felt as if they were having the same nightmare twice in one night.

'Oh, no, not again,' groaned Jo.

Summers went to the phone. 'I'd better see what's happening.' He rattled the receiver rest. 'Operator? Operator? Look, will someone put me through to the Governor – '

An electronic screech pierced his ears, and he staggered back, dropping the phone. 'What the devil . . .'

'Come on,' said Jo. 'We'd better get out of here.'

As they moved to the door it opened, revealing Vosper, an automatic pistol in his hand. He advanced towards Jo, smiling evilly. 'There's no escape this time, love. We've taken over the whole prison . . .'

The Master stood on the top of the steps, looking around him in satisfaction, as dead or unconscious prison warders were stripped of their uniforms and locked away out of sight.

Armed prisoners were disguising themselves as warders, revelling in their new roles. Already, fake warders had taken over the security arrangements at the main gate.

The Master smiled, rubbing his hands. 'Now then, Doctor, I'm ready for you!'

9

The Test

The Doctor drove up to the main gate and submitted to the usual rigmarole with spy-camera and pass. It seemed to take a little longer this time for some reason.

The gate was opened and as the Doctor drove under the arch, a uniformed figure jumped into the back of the car and jabbed a rifle at his head.

'Don't point that thing at me!' said the Doctor indignantly. 'I'm here on official business. I understand there's been some trouble in here.'

'That's right, and you're in it. Now, let's get this heap inside.'

Suddenly the Doctor realised that the man wasn't a warder, he was a prisoner. Calmly the Doctor moved the rifle-barrel out of line with his head. 'I was going there anyway,' he said with dignity, and drove along the ring-road towards the inner courtyard.

The main door clanged shut behind him.

A few minutes later, armed prisoners were shoving the Doctor into the Governor's office.

The figure at the desk was turned away from him. Suddenly the swivel chair swung round, revealing the face of the Master. He waved the prisoners away. 'All right, Vosper, Mailer . . .'

The Doctor dropped into a chair. 'Yes, I thought as much.'

The Master looked disappointed. 'You don't seem very surprised?'

'Hardly. How's the riot going?'

'Long since over,' said the Master proudly. 'I now have control of the entire prison.'

'And where's Jo Grant?'

'In our best cell.'

'Is she indeed?' The Doctor leaned forward. 'If you so much as touch a hair on her head, I'll . . .'

Suddenly there was a gun in the Master's hand. 'You'll do nothing, Doctor, or I'll put bullets through both your hearts.'

The Doctor raised a hand in temporary surrender. 'All right, all right. Why the delay – I take it I'm to be killed eventually?'

'Eventually, yes, Doctor. But for the moment, I need your help.'

'To control that Machine of yours – Professor Keller? You want to be careful, one day it'll end up killing you.'

'Oh, it won't harm me,' said the Master boastfully. 'I created it, after all. But I admit, it has developed something of a will of its own. You, I am sure, have the ability to control it – while I am engaged on other business.'

'What other business?'

'Your UNIT friends, Doctor, are transporting a nerve-gas missile. I intend to take it away from them.'

The Doctor shook his head. 'It's a lunatic-sounding scheme – still, I suppose that's only to be expected.'

The Master smiled. 'Come now, Doctor, let's not be petty. How can I fail? I launch the missile, wipe out the Peace Conference, the great Powers will blame each other and the world will be at war.'

The Master leaned back, preening himself – and the Doctor tipped the desk over on top of him.

Cat-quick reflexes enabled the Master to avoid being

pinned down. But the effort cost him his balance and he crashed over backwards on his chair.

Gun in hand he scrambled to his feet – and slipped and fell in the pool of water from the Governor's overturned carafe. He scrambled to his feet again, saw a cloaked figure looming over him and fired . . .

There was a hollow clang. The Doctor had whipped off his cape and draped it over the suit of armour in the corner. Before the Master could recover from his surprise, the Doctor was disappearing through the door.

The Master started to follow, changed his mind, ran to the window and shouted to Mailer, who was patrolling on top of the wall. 'The Doctor's escaping – stop him!'

Mailer waved an acknowledgement – and suddenly the Doctor shot out of a doorway and began sprinting across the courtyard.

Mailer threw his rifle to his shoulder and fired. The bullet kicked up dust at the Doctor's heels. Immediately he began zig-zagging wildly, dodging in and out amongst the parked vehicles.

Mailer fired again, and yet again.

A final burst of speed, and the Doctor disappeared through an arched doorway on the other side of the yard.

The Master turned from the window and hurried away.

The Doctor ran along the corridors towards the Special Wing. 'Our best cell' could only mean the condemned cell, and that was close to the Process Chamber.

'Jo,' he called. 'Jo, are you there?'

In the condemned cell, Jo and Doctor Summers were listening at the door.

Jo looked up at Summers. 'I'm sure I heard gunfire.'

'Perhaps some of the prison officers are still holding out.'

'Either that, or the Doctor's arrived!'

80

They heard the Doctor's voice.

'Jo! Jo, are you there?'

Jo put her lips to the peephole in the door. 'Is that you, Doctor? We're here – in the condemned cell.'

Faintly the Doctor heard Jo's voice. 'All right, Jo,' he called. 'I'm coming!'

Just as the Doctor was passing the Process Chamber, Mailer appeared at the end of the corridor. He saw the Doctor, raised his rifle and fired.

The Doctor ducked, spun to one side, and shot through the open doors of the Process Chamber.

In the condemned cell, Jo heard the shot. 'Doctor,' she called. 'Doctor, are you all right?'

Silence.

In the Process Chamber all was dark and silent.

The squat, sinister bulk of the Keller Machine dominated the far end of the room. The Doctor took a few steps towards it.

A voice behind him said, 'I rather thought you'd make for here, Doctor.'

The Doctor turned and saw the Master stepping from behind the door.

'Did you now?' said the Doctor coolly.

Mailer ran through the doorway. At the sight of the Doctor, he raised his rifle . . .

'No, no, Mailer,' said the Master reprovingly. 'Give me that.' He took the rifle from Mailer's hands. 'Now, show our patient to the chair, and handcuff him in.'

The Doctor considered resistance, but the combination of Mailer, the Master and the loaded rifle was just too formidable. And as long as the Master wanted him alive . . .

The Doctor sat in the Keller Machine chair, and Mailer handcuffed his wrists together behind him.

Satisfied that the Doctor couldn't move, Mailer stepped back.

'Thank you, Mailer,' said the Master urbanely. 'Now then, Doctor, I've effected some necessary repairs and adjustments to the Machine, and I'm about to try an experiment. I believe you can resist the influence of my Machine – at least for a time.'

'May I ask the purpose of this charade?'

'A test, Doctor, to see how long you can hold out.' The Master began searching the Doctor's pockets. 'Now, I'm sure you'll have it here somewhere . . . ah, good.' He produced the telepathic amplifier that the Doctor had taken from Chin Lee. 'This device, as you know, transmits and amplifies the power of the Machine. It can also be adjusted – like this – to turn that power against the wearer.' Making a quick adjustment to the device, the Master slipped it behind the Doctor's ear.

The Master went over to the control console. 'You'd better get out, Mailer.'

Thankfully, Mailer left the room. For all his toughness, Harry Mailer was suddenly very scared. There was something about the Master which made him feel that his own criminal career was no more significant than the tantrums of a child.

The Master's hands moved over the controls, and the Keller Machine began throbbing with life.

The Master backed away. 'I should like to stay and witness your nightmares, Doctor.'

'Then why don't you?' taunted the Doctor.

'I have business elsewhere,' said the Master, and hurried from the room.

'Too scared to stay,' thought the Doctor, then winced as his mind was engulfed in a sudden wave of fear.

The box was throbbing with energy now, and its electronic pulsing shook the entire room.

First came the flames. The Doctor braced himself. The flames weren't real, the terror of the Inferno was past.

A huge-eyed reptilian snout swam towards him out of the fire. A Silurian . . . Instinctively the Doctor shrank back.

The Silurian faded and a Dalek swum towards him . . . its harsh metallic voice grating inside his head. '*Exterminate! Exterminate! Exterminate!*'

It too faded, only to be replaced by the tall silver form of a Cyberman . . . then a War Machine . . .

Monster after monster, terror after terror from the Doctor's past loomed up to attack him.

The Doctor could have dealt with any one of them, after all he'd met and defeated them all before . . . But the steady, unremitting parade of horrors, combined with the atmosphere of pure fear generated by the Machine was eventually too much even for the Doctor . . .

Suddenly panic overtook him. For a moment he writhed in vain against the bondage of the steel hand-cuffs – then his body gave a convulsive jerk and his head fell back.

10

The Mind Parasite

The terror generated by the Keller Machine was spreading through the prison in waves.

The Master forced his way through a little group of escaped prisoners. They had dropped their weapons and were crouched on the floor, moaning with terror.

The Machine, the Master realised, was as big a menace to his allies as to his enemies. It *had* to be controlled. It took all the strength of his ferociously determined will for the Master to force himself to return along the corridor to the Process Chamber. He lifted the bar on the door and went inside.

Once inside, the Machine was still pulsing with evil power. The Master hurried to the console and tried frantically to close it down. After a moment the electronic pulsing ceased . . .

He hurried over to the Doctor who lay slackly in his chair, head lolling back. The Master studied him for a moment with what looked curiously like concern. He snatched up a stethoscope and listened to the Doctor's hearts. First the left one – nothing. Then the right – and here there was a feeble but steady beat.

The Master thumped the Doctor very hard on his chest, directly over the left hand heart. He thumped him a second time, and used the stethoscope to listen once more.

Now the left hand heart was beating too, slowly at first, then with increasing vigour.

Harry Mailer came cautiously into the room. 'Is he dead?'

'Not quite. You'd better wait outside.'

Mailer left.

The Master stood looking thoughtfully down at the Doctor.

The door to the condemned cell was flung open and Vosper beckoned to Doctor Summers. 'All right, you, out! You're being transferred to another cell.'

'Why me? What about Miss Grant?'

'She stays here, lucky girl. Luxury cell, all to herself.' Vosper nodded to the convict behind him. 'All right, Charlie, get him!'

Charlie, a burly, brutal type, grabbed Summers by the arm and dragged him out.

'I won't go without Miss Grant,' shouted Summers. 'Why don't you let us go back to the medical wing – we could do some good there . . .'

His protests ignored, he was dragged off down the corridor.

Jo looked at Vosper. 'What's so special about me?'

'We're saving you for the Machine,' said Vosper, and slammed the door.

The Doctor stirred, moaned and opened his eyes - to find the Master looking down at him.

'Doctor, Doctor – welcome back! Would it surprise you to know that one of your hearts had actually stopped? You were within seconds of death.'

The Doctor's voice was so faint as to be almost inaudible. 'You wanted to find out if I could hold out against that thing. Well, the answer is, I can't. No one can.'

'If I can control it from the console, Doctor, so can you.'

'No,' whispered the Doctor. 'No . . .'

'Come now, Doctor, we are both Time Lords.'

'I know the secret of that Machine. Inside it there is an alien creature. A mind parasite. It feeds on the evil in the mind. Soon it will feed on the evil in yours.'

'Nonsense,' said the Master uneasily. 'We can control it – we must!' He raised his voice, 'Mailer!'

Mailer reappeared in the doorway. 'Yeah?'

The Master nodded towards the Doctor. 'Release him and put him in the condemned cell with Miss Grant.' He leaned over the Doctor. 'Now, listen to me, Doctor. Unless you do as I ask, Miss Grant will be next in line for processing. All right, Mailer, take him out!'

Mailer unlocked the Doctor's handcuffs, and heaved him to his feet.

The Doctor was so feeble that Mailer had almost to carry him along the corridor to the condemned cell. 'Come on, Doctor,' he jeered. 'Your feet are dragging.'

Suddenly the Doctor rallied. Flinging Mailer aside he made a desperate attempt to escape.

Vosper, who had been waiting by the door of the condemned cell, darted forwards and clubbed the Doctor with his pistol.

As the Doctor fell, Mailer raised his rifle like a club for a second, savage blow. A voice snapped 'No!'

The Master was standing at the end of the corridor. 'I happen to need the Doctor in one piece. Put him in the cell!'

Vosper unlocked the cell door. Mailer heaved the Doctor to his feet and shoved him inside. He staggered a few paces forward, and then fell.

As Jo ran to help him, a familiar voice spoke from the doorway. 'Good evening, Miss Grant. A great pleasure to see you again.'

Jo turned round in astonishment. 'Master! What are you doing here?'

'The Doctor will explain – when he recovers. Try to make him see reason, my dear – for your own sake. Good night, Miss Grant.'

The Master stepped back, and the door closed behind him.

In the corridor, Mailer said, 'Why don't you turn him over to me and the boys? I'll have him eating out of your hand.'

'You don't know the Doctor. All you could do is kill him. I don't want him hurt – just guarded. I want an armed man on this door at all times.'

Vosper nodded. 'All right. I'll do it meself.'

'Mailer, I want the Special Wing completely cleared - except for those two in there.'

'What the hell for?'

'Don't argue, Mailer – *do it*!'

Mailer felt the force of the Master's will like a blast of heat. He nodded hastily. 'Yeah – okay, okay!'

'Good. Meet me in the Governor's office when you've finished.'

The Doctor was completely unconscious now, his breathing very shallow.

Jo jumped up and hammered frantically on the cell door. 'You out there – please, listen to me!'

'Oh, go to sleep, darling.'

'Please, open the door!'

There was a moment's silence. Then to Jo's vast relief there was a rattle of keys and the door was flung open.

Vosper looked down at Jo, who was kneeling by the Doctor. 'Proper little Miss Nightingale, ain't you?'

'Look at him,' said Jo indignantly. 'He needs a doctor.'

'Oh, what a shame!'

'At least help me to get him onto the bed. He's too heavy for me.'

Vosper helped Jo to heave the Doctor onto the bed.

Jo gave him her most winning smile. 'Thank you. Now will you get Doctor Summers – please?'

'Anything for you, darling,' said Vosper wearily.

He left the cell.

The Master stood in the Process Chamber staring down at the Keller Machine.

As the Doctor had finally realised, it wasn't really a Machine at all, but a prison for an alien entity that fed on men's minds. Now it looked as if the creature was growing strong enough to break out of its prison.

As if sensing the Master's presence, the Machine began to throb. 'You can't harm me,' said the Master contemptuously. 'I'm too strong for you.'

The throbbing increased.

'I brought you here,' shouted the Master. 'I gave you the minds you need to feed on. You are *my* servant.'

An electronic pulsing filled the room.

The Master ran to the console and frantically operated controls – without the slightest effect. The creature had grown so strong that the force-field controlled from the console could no longer restrain it.

Angrily the Master glared at the Machine. Inside the central column the strange sponge-like shape was pulsating steadily. 'I'm too strong for you!'

The Machine blurred, shimmered – and turned into the Doctor.

But no ordinary Doctor. This Doctor was a giant, towering high above the Master.

The giant Doctor threw back his head and laughed, peal upon peal of mocking laughter.

'No!' screamed the Master. 'No!'

The creature in the Machine had plucked the Master's

one great fear out of his mind. His fear of the Doctor, of the Doctor's mockery, of the way that the Doctor could always make him feel small.

Summoning all his will-power, the Master turned and staggered from the Process Chamber. He slammed the door shut and lowered the locking bar into place. For a moment he leaned gasping against the door. 'No more human minds for you to feed on,' he muttered savagely. 'We'll see what starvation does to bring you to heel.'

Summers concluded his examination of the Doctor and looked up at Jo in total puzzlement. 'It's extraordinary. Quite extraordinary. His whole physical make-up just isn't human.'

Jo said impatiently. 'I know. What's the *matter* with him?'

'He's been beaten up, physically and mentally. It's as if his system has suffered some enormous shock. He seems to be in a kind of coma.'

'Can't you do anything for him.'

'I very much doubt it.' Summers took a bottle from his pocket, and shook a couple of pills into Jo's hand. 'You might try giving him these if he recovers consciousness.' He leaned forward. 'Miss Grant, do you have any idea who organised this second break?'

Before Jo could answer, Vosper came back into the cell. 'All right, Doc, time's up.' He nodded down at the still unconscious Doctor. 'What's the verdict? Is he done for?'

Summers rose. 'Not quite, though it's no thanks to you.'

'Come on, Doc. Don't forget to send in your bill.'

He shoved Summers out into the corridor, and the cell door was closed once more.

The Doctor stirred and muttered something. Jo hurried to his side with the pills. 'Here, Doctor, take these.'

Feebly he shook his head. 'No, Jo, wrong metabolism . . . probably kill me. I'll be all right . . . just need . . . rest.'

His head fell back, and his eyes closed. Within minutes he had sunk back into his coma – a coma that seemed to Jo very close to death.

The Master sat behind the Governor's desk still shaken from his ordeal – as Harry Mailer noticed as soon as he entered the room.

'You all right?'

'Yes, of course.'

'Well, you don't look too good to me.' Mailer sat down on the other side of the desk.

The Master made a mighty effort to rally himself. He was controlling this gang of vicious thugs by little more than the force of his will. He couldn't afford to show any signs of weakness. When he spoke again, it was in his usual authoritative manner. 'I want an armed guard on the door of the Process Chamber. No one is to go near that Machine.'

'Don't worry, mate. None of my lot are likely to.'

The Master stroked his beard. 'Perhaps not – but morbid curiosity can be very strong. See to it, will you?'

'Yeah, okay.'

The Master smiled, bringing to bear the full force of his personality. 'I am pleased with you, Mailer. You have done very well. Very well indeed.'

'Good. Then perhaps you'll do something for me?'

'Anything!' said the Master expansively. 'You have only to ask.'

'Maybe you'll explain why we don't all scarper – tonight, before it gets light?'

'My dear Mailer, you're simply not thinking. A gang of armed convicts roaming the countryside . . .'

'We can get hold of civvies – and there's cars outside.'

'Even so, you must remember that you'd have not only the police but the army against you. Dogs, troops, helicopters. I assure you, you'd all be captured or killed before tomorrow morning.'

Mailer looked suspiciously at him. 'I take it you've got a better idea?'

'Of course,' said the Master confidently. Drawing the curtains, he pulled down a wall screen, then crossed to a slide projector, set up on a nearby table. 'How would you like a free pardon, unlimited money, and a plane ticket to anywhere in the world?'

'How would I like it – do me a favour!'

'Then pay attention.' The Master clicked on the projector and a picture filled the screen. It showed a giant rocket, loaded on to a transporter. 'This is Thunderbolt, a nerve gas missile, nuclear powered, and British, of course.'

'Of course!' muttered Mailer.

'And what's more, it's illegal,' continued the Master. 'Gas warfare was banned several years ago. The British Government have therefore decided to dump this missile at sea.' The Master paused impressively. 'Tomorrow morning, the missile, with a very small escort, will pass within a very few miles of this prison.'

'I suppose you want me to hijack it,' said Mailer sarcastically.

'Right first time! I intend to aim the missile at the Peace Conference in London.'

Mailer shook his head in amazement. 'You've got to be joking.'

'I assure you I am not.'

The Master flicked on another slide and a map appeared on the screen.

He pointed. 'Now, this is the prison . . . and this is where you will ambush the convoy . . .'

* * *

91

When Vosper opened the cell door to check on his prisoners, the Doctor was still stretched out unconscious.

Jo was fast asleep in a chair beside the bed. Her eyes opened as the cell door opened.

Vosper nodded towards the Doctor. 'He's still with us, then?'

Jo yawned. 'Sorry you're disappointed.'

'You watch your lip,' growled Vosper.

'How about some breakfast?'

'What do you think this is – a holiday camp?'

'He's not going to be much use to the Master if he doesn't get some food, is he? You weren't told to starve us to death, were you?'

'All right, all right,' said Vosper, worn down yet again by Jo's insistence. He called outside the cell. 'Charlie, nip along to the kitchens and rustle up some grub.' He looked down at the Doctor. 'Though from the look of your mate here, I very much doubt if he's going to need it.'

He went out, slamming the door behind him.

The Doctor opened his eyes and sat up, beaming at the astonished Jo. 'Well done, my dear. Now maybe we can do something about getting out of here.'

In the courtyard, a ragged line of armed prisoners was assembling by the prison's Black Maria, watched by Mailer and the Master. Having finally convinced Mailer that his scheme was a practical one, the Master was now using all his eloquence to convince Mailer's men.

'And remember,' he concluded, 'if you succeed, this operation will be your passport to prosperity and freedom - anywhere in the world. Good luck to you all!'

Naturally, the Master was lying. He had told them that once the missile was in his hands he intended to use it to blackmail the Government, gaining free pardons and millions in cash for them all to share.

But in fact, the Master had no such intention. Once the missile was in his hands, he intended to fire it, bringing all the horrors of war upon the world.

Once that happened, the Master would no longer be concerned with the fate of Mailer and his men – or indeed, with that of the entire population of the Earth.

Unaware that he was no more than a disposable pawn in the Master's schemes, Mailer shouted, 'Everyone got the picture? Right then, let's go!'

They all climbed into the Black Maria and it drove away.

11

Hijack

The cell door opened and Vosper came in, followed by
Charlie, who was carrying a tray which held two mugs of
tea and a plate of toast.

There wasn't a lot of toast left, and Charlie and
Vosper were munching as they entered the cell.

'I thought that was supposed to be for us,' said Jo
indignantly. She was sitting by the Doctor's bed. The
Doctor was stretched out as before, apparently unconscious.

'Don't worry,' growled Charlie. 'You'll get yours.'

'Thanks,' said Jo and high-kicked the tray upwards
into his face.

Charlie staggered back, spluttering and soaked with
hot tea. The Doctor sprang to his feet and felled him with
a swift touch of Venusian Aikido.

Vosper jumped back, reaching for his gun. The Doctor
snatched up the heavy metal tray and crowned him with
it. There was a satisfying *bong* and Vosper fell, and Jo
snatched up his pistol.

The Doctor and Jo shot out through the still-open
door. The keys were still in the lock, and the Doctor
locked the cell and tossed the keys along the corridor.

Jo was looking at him in amazement. 'Really Doctor
for someone who was at death's door a moment ago – '

'Yes, I do have remarkable powers of recovery, don't
I?' said the Doctor cheerfully. 'Come along.'

As they hurried along the corridor, they could hear Vosper and Charlie, obviously recovering, banging on the cell door and yelling for help . . .

The Doctor led Jo swiftly along the prison corridors and into the Governor's office. Their luck was in, and they met nobody on the way. The big old-fashioned room was empty. The Doctor noticed that someone had picked the desk up, and cleared up most of the mess.

Jo went over to the window. Armed prisoners were running around the courtyard. 'They seem to be organising a search for us.'

'They'll be expecting us to try and break out, Jo!'

'Well, aren't we?'

The Doctor shook his head. 'Not while everybody is chasing about. We'll let 'em cool off a bit and try later.'

'Telephone!' said Jo suddenly. 'There must be a telephone somewhere.'

'There is,' said the Doctor, pointing to a box on the desk. 'It's a prison telephone, they keep it in a locked box. Anyway, they've got prisoners manning the switchboard.'

Thwarted, Jo wandered over to the projector and switched it on. A map appeared on the wall screen. She fiddled with the projector, and the map was replaced by a picture of a rocket on its trailer. 'What's that?'

The Doctor glanced at the screen. 'That, my dear Jo' is the Thunderbolt missile, at present under the escort of Captain Yates.'

'What's it got to do with the Master?'

'Everything,' said the Doctor simply. 'He's hoping to steal it!'

Following the Master's plan, Mailer and his men had parked the Black Maria in a country lane just off the main road.

The spot chosen for the ambush was ideal. The road narrowed slightly at this point, running between high grassy banks lined with trees. Mailer posted his men in cover on both sides of the road. 'Now, don't forget,' he ordered. 'Wait till they get level before you let them have it.'

They waited - and in a surprisingly short time there came the thin whine of motor bike engines and the rumble of a heavy vehicle. 'Right, here they come!'

The convoy was a sitting duck – or rather, it was like the row of ducks in a shooting gallery.

First came the two motor cyclists. Then the Land Rover, with Mike Yates and a UNIT driver. Then the heavy transporter with Benton at the wheel. Then two more motor cyclists bringing up the rear.

As the little convoy trundled along, Mike Yates was thinking that things seemed to be running smoothly at last. They had been held up for an incredibly long time because the crane needed to put the rocket onto the trailer had failed to arrive.

When it did arrive at last, getting the rocket onto the loader and securing it safely had been an incredibly slow and complicated business. Only by driving through the night had the convoy managed to get back on schedule.

Nevertheless, they *were* back on schedule, and should make the rendezvous point in Portsmouth in plenty of time. After that the Navy could take over the Thunderbolt missile and, as far as Mike Yates was concerned, they were welcome to it.

Mike was in the middle of these consoling thoughts when the first bullets struck the jeep. His driver slumped over the wheel and the jeep careered wildly across the road.

Conscious of the rattle of bullets all around him, Mike grabbed the wheel and managed to run the Land

Rover into the side of the road, where it hit the bank with a thump that almost stunned him.

The motor cyclists had no chance at all.

In the open and unprotected, they were cut down by a hail of bullets from both sides of the road. Caught in a crossfire, they toppled from their machines and lay dead or wounded scattered over the road and up the bank. Upturned motor cycles roared and whined, spinning their wheels . . .

Benton put his foot on the gas, hoping to crash straight through the ambush. Suddenly a black van swung out in front of him.

Instinctively, Benton jammed on the brakes and the heavy transporter slewed into the bank at the side of the road. Benton started to climb out, reaching for his revolver. Suddenly the door was flung open, and the butt of a pistol smashed down on his head.

His unconscious body was dragged out into the road and a convict took his place.

Mike Yates meanwhile had already scrambled out of the jeep and taken cover behind a tree at the side of the road. His first responsibility was to get a message out, and he was talking frantically into his UNIT walkie-talkie. 'Venus to Jupiter, Venus to Jupiter, do you read me? Convoy under armed attack . . . Estimated position . . .'

On the other side of the road, one of the prisoners spotted the khaki-clad figure, raised his rifle and fired.

The bullet didn't hit Mike Yates but it hit the intercom, which flew through the air. Mike gave a realistic yell of agony, spun round and collapsed. Satisfied, the prisoner moved away. Mike edged towards the walkie-talkie . . .

Jupiter, which was of course UNIT HQ, had got only the first part of Mike's message, before it was cut off.

The Brigadier was shouting into the radio-telephone. 'Jupiter to Venus, Jupiter to Venus, give us your position . . .'

The only reply was a crackling of static.

Mike Yates was fiddling frantically with the walkie-talkie, 'Venus to Jupiter – do you read me?'

The little unit was completely dead, its casing shattered by the bullet.

Cautiously, Mike raised his head and looked round – and saw the transporter being driven away, with the Black Maria following.

The hijack had been a complete success.

Since he'd already lost the missile, Mike decided grimly, the only thing to do was to find out where it was being taken.

As the transporter disappeared, Mike looked round and spotted an apparently undamaged motor-bike. It lay at the side of the road, engine roaring, the dead rider huddled nearby.

Mike ran to the motor-bike, lifted it upright, swung into the saddle and sped off down the road after the stolen missile.

Laying by the roadside, Sergeant Benton raised his head and stared dazedly at Mike Yates roaring away . . . then he fell back unconscious.

The Brigadier pointed at the map. 'Last time Captain Yates checked in officially, he was – here. Now, given the estimated speed of the convoy and the time of the emergency call, the ambush must have taken place about – here! I want a chopper standing by to take me down there as soon as possible!'

Corporal Bell said, 'I'll get on to it right away, sir.'

'And I want a Mobile HQ and a full forensic team in the area.'

She reached for the phone. 'Shall we ask for police and Regular Army co-operation, sir?'

'No. UNIT personnel only. This missile isn't supposed to exist, remember! Keep trying to get in touch with Captain Yates.'

Corporal Bell returned to the radio-telephone. 'Jupiter to Venus. Do you read me?' But there was no reply.

At that precise moment Captain Yates was lying in the grass at the edge of what appeared to be a deserted airfield.

The transporter had been parked outside the hangar doors, and a little group of men – who, to Mike's amazement wore Army uniform – were busy with a mobile crane, preparing to set the missile up, ready for firing. Mike decided he had seen enough. It was more important than ever that he passed on the location of the missile to UNIT HQ.

He turned and sprinted back to where he had left the motor bike, lifted it up and swung into the saddle, kicking the engine into life. Unfortunately, the noise attracted the attention of one of the armed convicts.

As Mike sped away, the convict opened fire, and several of his fellows joined in.

This time Mike Yates wasn't so lucky. One of the bullets struck him in the shoulder, smashing him from the motor-bike.

Mike lay still for some minutes, sick and dazed from the wound and from the heavy fall.

Gamely he started to struggle to his feet, but it was already too late. There was a pounding of feet, and a gang of armed convicts ran up. Brutally they hauled him to his feet, and dragged him away.

The Brigadier was trying to get some sense out of a still-dazed Sergeant Benton, while a UNIT medical orderly dressed the gash on the top of the Sergeant's head. All around, the UNIT team were taking away the dead and wounded, clearing wreckage, and searching the scene for clues.

'And is that all you can tell me, Benton?' said the Brigadier at last.

'It all happened so quickly, sir,' said Benton. He looked apologetically at the Brigadier.

'Did you see what happened to Captain Yates?'

'I thought they got him, sir.'

'Not unless they took the body with them. And one of the bikes was missing.'

'I saw someone on a motor-bike, sir – just before I passed out again. Maybe it was Captain Yates. Maybe he followed them, sir?'

'Yes, maybe. Anything else, Benton?'

'There is just one other thing, sir. They were using a plain black van, the sort the police use. A black Maria.'

The Brigadier raised his voice. 'Map!'

A UNIT corporal hurried up with a map. The Brigadier studied it for a moment. 'Stangmoor Prison!'

Benton looked puzzled. 'What's that, sir?'

'Where else would you get a Black Maria? Benton, you stay here and rendezvous with Major Cosgrove and the mobile HQ. I'll join you later.'

'Where will you be, sir?'

'I'm going to take a look at Stangmoor prison!'

The Brigadier headed for his helicopter.

Jo was still staring out of the window.

The Doctor sat at the Governor's desk, brooding, his chin in his hands.

Jo swung round. 'Doctor, we can't just go on sitting here.'

'Why not? It's the safest place at the moment. Besides,

100

I need time to think. I've got to find a way of dealing with that creature.'

'What creature?'

'The one in the machine.'

'You mean there's something alive in there?'

'I do.'

'What is it?'

'An alien mind parasite, Jo, a creature from another planet. It feeds on mental energy, particularly on the mind's darker, more primitive impulses. On evil, if you like. It's probably the deadliest threat to mankind since the beginning of time . . .'

The Doctor sat staring into space, thinking of the remote planet on the edge of a far distant galaxy where the creatures had first been discovered.

No expedition had ever returned from that terrible planet. Incredibly cunning and ferociously powerful, the mind parasites drained the energy of any intelligent beings they encountered.

The Master had brought one here, imprisoned in a force-field, disguised as a Machine, to serve his own evil purposes. Judging by his eagerness to pass on the care of the creature to the Doctor, it was rapidly growing too strong for him.

Jo wandered back to the window. 'Doctor, look. It's the Master. He seems to be leaving.'

Peering cautiously through the window curtains, the Doctor saw the Master standing by his black limousine, having a last word with Mailer – who, in turn, seemed to have just arrived in a Black Maria, with a number of other convicts.

The Master got into the limousine, and it drove away.

'Right,' said the Doctor. 'Now's our chance!'

Jo nodded eagerly. 'We can slip out by the hospital and through the rear courtyard.'

'I didn't mean our chance to escape, Jo. I meant my

101

chance to get into the Process Chamber, and destroy the creature in the Machine.'

'I see.'

Jo tried to hand over the gun she had taken from Vosper, but the Doctor waved it away.

'You keep it, Jo, you're trained to use those things. They only make me nervous.'

They hurried out.

After a good deal of banging and shouting, Charlie and Vosper had been released by a passing fellow prisoner.

Charlie had promptly got hold of a gun, and gone off in search of the Doctor, the blow with the tray still very fresh in his mind, with a headache and a bump on his head to make sure he didn't forget.

His search of the corridors and courtyards had been fruitless, and now he was returning towards the Process Chamber in case the Doctor had taken refuge there.

Suddenly the air in front of him seemed to ripple with a blood-red glow. It cleared, and there was the Keller Machine in the middle of the corridor. It was throbbing angrily.

Charlie stared in astonishment - and screamed as the mind parasite sucked his mental energy, his very life force, out of his mind and body with a dreadful voracious hunger.

Charlie fell dead, no more than an empty husk.

The air shimmered and the Machine disappeared.

A few minutes later the Doctor and Jo came hurrying along the corridor and almost stumbled over the body.

The Doctor knelt to examine it.

'Look at his face,' whispered Jo. 'He must have been terrified, just like the others.'

The Doctor rose. 'Yes. Perhaps the creature has learned to move.'

'How?'

'Teleportation. Come on, Jo.'

They hurried down the corridor and went into the Process Chamber. The Machine was gone.

'You were right, Doctor,' whispered Jo.

A voice said, 'Drop the gun, girly.'

Vosper and Mailer were standing in the doorway. Both were armed.

Mailer raised his heavy automatic. 'I think I've had just about enough of you.'

The Doctor began talking, in the hope of distracting Mailer. 'Maybe so, but before you pull that trigger, I think I should warn you – '

Suddenly the Doctor broke off.

He stared over Mailer's shoulder, eyes widening in horror.

'What's the matter with you?' snarled Mailer.

'Look behind you!'

'I've heard that one before.'

'Look behind you!' whispered the Doctor.

Such was the urgency in his voice that Mailer turned.

The Keller Machine was materialising in the corridor behind Vosper.

Hearing the throbbing, Vosper swung round, and fired a shot at the Machine. It sucked him towards it like a magnet, held him writhing and screaming for a moment, dropped the discarded body and disappeared.

The Doctor swept Jo into hiding behind the console, while Mailer had flattened himself against the wall just outside the door.

When the Machine vanished, Jo and the Doctor emerged cautiously from hiding.

There was a throbbing sound, a blood-red glow, and the Keller Machine materialised in front of them . . .

12

The Escape

For a moment Jo and the Doctor stood motionless.

The Machine was throbbing, and they could feel its power, drawing them towards it.

Suddenly Mailer sprang through the doorway. One hand was clutching his forehead, the other held an automatic. Face twisted with terror, he fired wildly at the Machine, then turned and fled down the corridor.

The Machine shimmered and disappeared.

'What happened, Doctor?' gasped Jo. 'Why did it just go away?'

'I don't think we can have tempted its appetite sufficiently.'

'Why not?'

'I imagine it detected a higher concentration of evil in Mailer. Something to be said for a pure mind after all!'

Jo shivered. 'I think we'd better get out of here before it comes back for us.'

She went out into the corridor, and the Doctor followed. There was no sign of Mailer or the Keller Machine. Instead they saw Barnham, wandering distractedly towards them in his striped hospital pyjamas and dressing gown.

'Barnham!' exclaimed Jo. 'What are you doing here?'

He gave her his confused, child-like smile. 'I was looking for you. I heard this noise.'

Jo took his arm. 'Well, you come with us. Don't worry we're getting away from here.'

'But I didn't understand.'

The Doctor turned to Jo. 'Come on, we've got to stop the Master from launching that Missile.' He patted Barnham on the shoulder. 'Don't worry, old chap, just you come with us!'

The UNIT helicopter droned over Stangmoor Prison, hanging in the air like a great metal dragonfly.

The Brigadier studied the peaceful scene below. Occasional blue clad figures strolled across the courtyards, the scattering of parked vehicles looked like toys against the grey stone bulk of the prison . . .

He spoke into his intercom. 'Windmill 347 to Trap Four. Do you read me?'

A crisp voice came through the headphones. 'Trap Four to Windmill 347 reading you loud and clear.'

The voice belonged to Major Cosgrove, who had been assigned to help the Brigadier on this operation.

Cosgrove was the new academic type of soldier. He was neat, bespectacled, intelligent and quite unbearably efficient. He sat in the UNIT mobile HQ parked a few miles from the prison, listening to the Brigadier's voice.

'Major Cosgrove, reading you loud and clear,' he repeated. 'Any results, sir? Over.'

'I'm over Stangmoor Prison now, Major. No sign of the missile and everything seems quiet and normal.'

'Are you going to land, sir? Over.'

'No, I don't think so. I know I said everything seems normal, but I'm quite sure it's not. I'll continue the recce for the moment. Over and out.'

The Doctor, Jo and Barnham had reached a door that led to the courtyard.

The Doctor opened it cautiously. 'Nobody about. Come on, Jo, let's take a look outside. Barnham, you'd better stay here.'

They moved cautiously out into the courtyard. Jo leading the way. She heard a droning sound, looked upwards, and immediately began capering up and down, waving her arms. 'Look, Doctor, it's a UNIT helicopter.'

Jo went on waving frantically. Caught up in her enthusiasm, the Doctor started waving, too.

From behind them a harsh voice said, 'All right, you two, back inside!'

Two armed convicts had appeared in the corridor behind them. Reluctantly Jo and the Doctor went back inside the prison.

The bigger of the two convicts, a balding thug called Fuller, jabed them with his rifle to hurry them along. 'I said back inside, come on!'

Suddenly Fuller found the massive figure of Barnham looming over him.

'Don't hurt them,' said Barnham in an unhappy voice.

Fuller tried to shove him away with the rifle, but Barnham grabbed the weapon in one enormous hand and shoved it across Fuller's throat. 'I said don't hurt them.'

The Doctor saw that the bemused smaller convict was raising his weapon to fire.

Hurriedly he pulled Barnham away. 'It's all right, old chap. Let's get out of here, shall we?'

Reluctantly Barnham let go of the rifle. 'He was going to hurt you,' he complained.

'It's all right,' said Jo soothingly, and Barnham allowed himself to be led away.

In the Governor's office Mailer, who had somehow managed to elude the Keller Machine, was talking to the Master on the telephone. He was furiously angry. 'What do you mean, we messed things up. You got your missile, didn't you?'

The Master was speaking from a little office, built into one corner of the disused aircraft hangar. Beside him was Mike Yates, unconscious in a chair, his hands tied behind him.

'You left one of the UNIT people alive,' said the Master coldly. 'He followed you here. Fortunately he was caught.'

'Look, mate, I don't care about that,' said Mailer's impatient voice, 'I want you back here at Stang Moor right away.'

'That's quite impossible. I'm busy preparing the missile for launching.'

'I don't care how busy you are,' said Mailer furiously. '*You get back here*. That Machine of yours has broken loose. It's moving around the prison. It's killed Lenny Vosper, and it nearly killed me.'

'I tell you I can't leave.'

As far as the Master was concerned, the Machine could kill everyone in the prison and welcome. Mailer's next words forced him to think again. 'Now you listen to me, mate. My mob won't stay here with that thing on the loose. They'll start running, and I'll be running with them.'

'But you'll be caught.'

'Maybe so. But if I get caught, remember, so do you. They'll be asking where that missile is – and I just might tell them. Think about it.'

There was a click, as Mailer slammed down the phone.

The Master sighed. He really should have killed Mailer once he was no longer useful. It was always a mistake to be too compassionate. He turned to Mike Yates, and swung round the swivel chair so that his captive faced him. 'You can stop shamming unconsciousness, Captain Yates. I hope you're quite comfortable?'

Mike opened his eyes, still a little dazed from the combination of his wound, the fall, and the subsequent rough handling. 'Why?'

'Why did I take the missile? I intend to use it.'

'You'll never be able to fire it, it's too complex.'

The Master chuckled, glancing at the firing control console which he had already rigged up in the corner of the office hut.

'Nonsense. The mechanism is childishly simple. Besides, I have all the technical assistance I need.' He waved towards the open door of the hut, through which could be seen a team of uniformed men hard at work readying the missile for launching.

'I was going to ask you about those soldiers.'

'Hired mercenaries in faked uniforms. Everything's a matter of money these days, my dear Captain. Now, if you'll excuse me?'

The Master turned away, then paused in the doorway. 'Ah, yes, you're probably wondering why you are still alive?'

'It did cross my mind.'

'In the event – the extremely unlikely event – of your UNIT friends finding us before the missile is ready to fire, you will make a very useful hostage. Remember that!'

The Master left.

As soon as he was out of sight, Mike Yates set to work, sawing his bonds against the steel strut at the back of the chair. It was a slim chance, but so long as there was any chance at all he would go on trying.

Mailer looked disgustedly at the Doctor, Jo and Barnham. 'Well done, Fuller, where did you find 'em?'

'Outside in the courtyard,' said Fuller. 'Waving to a helicopter.'

'What? Did it see them?'

'Dunno. I don't think so. Anyway, it's cleared off now.'

Mailer looked uneasily at Barnham, who smiled back at him.

Mailer shivered, thinking of what he too might have become. 'Get that zombie out of here, he gives me the creeps.' One of the convicts led Barnham away. Mailer turned back to the Doctor. 'I don't know what we're going to do about you, Doctor.'

The Doctor leaned forward, and Mailer raised the automatic. 'Back off!'

'Mailer, *why* are you helping the Master?' demanded the Doctor.

'Simple. I'm helping him because he's helping me.'

'What did he promise you?'

'Money. A free pardon. A ticket to anywhere in the world.'

'Do you really believe he'll keep his promises?'

'Why not?'

'He doesn't care if you live or die,' said Jo. 'He's using you.'

Mailer shrugged. 'He's using me, I'm using him. Can you make me a better offer, Doc?'

The Doctor considered. 'Let us go free and I'll do my best for you.'

Mailer chuckled. 'Well, if that's your best offer, it really ain't good enough. All right, Fuller, wheel 'em out. Back to the condemned cell.'

The Brigadier was back in his mobile HQ with Major Cosgrove. 'I tell you I know exactly where that missile is, Major.' He pointed to a wall map with his swagger stick. 'Stangmoor Prison. It all adds up. Benton saw a Black Maria when the convoy was ambushed, and I saw the

Doctor and Miss Grant. The Master's taken over the prison and I'm convinced he's using it as a hideout for the missile.'

Cosgrove nodded. 'I assume we'll be taking the place, sir?'

'Major Cosgrove, have you ever *seen* Stangmoor Prison? It used to be an old fortress. You'd need an army to get in there.'

And for political reasons, thought the Brigadier, an army was just what they couldn't have. The place would have to be taken with his own relatively small force of UNIT troops.

Major Cosgrove was thinking hard. 'A fortress, you said, sir? I suppose there couldn't possibly be some kind of secret entrance – an underground tunnel, something like that?'

The Brigadier gave him a look.

Unperturbed, Cosgrove said, 'I've got a plan of the prison here, sir.'

Trust Cosgrove to have everything ready, thought the Brigadier. He studied the plan and blinked. 'It appears that you're right, Major Cosgrove.' He pointed to the map. 'There's a sort of underground passage, here. It doesn't lead into the prison itself of course, but it'll get us to the far side of the inner courtyard.'

Cosgrove beamed. 'I say, it's almost like something in a film, isn't it, sir?'

The Brigadier gave him another quelling look, and resumed his study of the map.

Suddenly a voice crackled from the RT 'Greyhound Seven to Trap One.'

Cosgrove flicked a switch. 'Go ahead, Trap One here.'

'I'm on observation at the prison gates, sir. A black limousine has just entered the prison. Bearded passenger in the back.'

'It must be the Master,' said the Brigadier. 'They

wouldn't let anyone else inside anyway. That settles it, Cosgrove, we're going to take that prison.'

'By using the underground passage, sir?'

'Yes,' said the Brigadier. To prove that Cosgrove didn't have a monopoly on good ideas, he added, 'And by using a Trojan horse!'

The Doctor and Jo were playing draughts in the condemned cell. The door was flung open and the Master appeared dramatically in the doorway. 'Ah, Doctor!'

The Doctor held a finger to his lips. 'Sssh!' He studied the board for a moment, then made his move, taking two of Jo's pieces. 'There!'

The Master wasn't used to being ignored. 'I was about to say, Doctor – '

'Ssh!' said Jo. She moved one of her pieces in a complicated zig-zag across the board, taking nearly all the Doctor's pieces, and conclusively winning the game. 'There!'

The Doctor rose and yawned. 'The trouble with this game is it's really too simple,' he said sulkily. 'I'm really only used to three-dimensional chess.'

He stretched out on the bed and lay back, his hands behind his head.

The Master sighed. 'All right, Doctor, I have allowed you your little gesture of defiance. Now perhaps we can talk seriously?'

'I suppose you're going to ask me to control that mind parasite for you?'

'I am.'

'Well, I can't. No one can.'

'You underestimate yourself, Doctor. I'm sure you are perfectly capable of controlling it – for a time at least.'

'Even if I could control it, why should I help you?'

'To save lives?' suggested the Master. 'A number of people have died already.'

'Most of them hard-case criminals who were helping you.'

'Very well then. To save one particular life.'

'My own?'

The Master shook his head. He stepped aside and Mailer came into the cell, the inevitable automatic in his hand. Fuller closed the door behind him.

The Master nodded, not towards the Doctor, but to Jo Grant.

'Don't take any notice of him, Doctor,' said Jo. 'He's bluffing.'

'Am I? I assure you, that unless the Doctor agrees to help me, Miss Grant, Mailer will shoot you. Here and now.'

Mailer cocked the automatic.

There was a long pause – at least, it seemed long to Jo Grant.

Then the Doctor rose, and began pacing thoughtfully about the cell. 'It's only a theory, but I think there may be a way to inhibit that Machine's power of movement.'

'You'll never have a better chance to put your theory to the test, Doctor.'

'Where is the thing now? Still wandering about?'

Mailer said, 'One of the lads said it's back in the Process Chamber.'

'Temporarily glutted no doubt,' said the Master. 'Well, Doctor?'

'I'll need a lot of equipment.'

'Stangmoor is a progressive prison, Doctor,' said the Master expansively. 'The contents of the Prison Workshop are at your disposal.'

'All right. I'll give it a try.'

The Doctor moved towards the door.

'All right, Fuller, let us out,' called the Master.

The door opened and Mailer, the Doctor and the Master left the cell.

Jo tried to follow but the Master barred her way. 'No, Miss Grant, you will remain here, as a guarantee of the Doctor's good behaviour.'

The Master stepped back, and the door was closed.

The Brigadier was giving a final briefing to Major Cosgrove and the two young officers who would be commanding the attack force. 'We shall, as you realise, be very considerably outnumbered. However, not all our opponents will be armed, and none of them will be trained soldiers.'

Cosgrove said brightly, 'And of course we will have surprise on our side.'

The Brigadier, who had planned to conclude his address with that point gave Cosgrove yet another quelling look. 'Exactly! Now, any questions?'

'No questions, sir,' said Cosgrove, before anyone else could speak.

The two young officers saluted and marched out.

'It's an excellent plan if I may say so, sir,' said Major Cosgrove. 'I should think there's a very good chance of success.'

'Thank you,' said the Brigadier drily. 'I'm very relieved.'

Cosgrove moved off to check the movement orders. There was a tap on the door and Benton appeared, a little pale but otherwise back to normal, apart from a patch of plaster on the crown of his head.

The Brigadier looked up. 'What the devil are you doing here, Benton? You're supposed to be in hospital.'

'I discharged myself, sir. I'm all right now, just a bit of a sore head.'

'Well, what do you want?'

'I'd like to come on the assault, sir.'

'Benton, for all we know you may be suffering from severe concussion – ' began the Brigadier.

'It's only a scratch, sir,' said Benton desperately. 'You always said I'd got a thick head. I'd just like a chance to get at the blokes who did it.'

The Brigadier nodded, accepting the inevitable. 'All right, Sergeant Benton. If you're sure you feel fit you can take charge of the underground assault party. Major Cosgrove will put you in the picture.'

Benton saluted. 'Thank you, sir.' He hesitated. 'I suppose there's no news of Captain Yates?'

'I'm sorry, Benton, there's nothing. Nothing at all.'

In the hangar office, Captain Yates was still sawing frantically at the ropes that tied his wrists. The strut had proved too smooth, but Mike had managed to get out of the chair, and he was trying his luck with the edge of an old metal table.

Suddenly, to his delight, the frayed strands of rope began to part – just as he heard footsteps coming towards the door . . .

13

The Attack

By the time the guard came back into the hut to check up on his prisoner, Mike Yates was slumped back in the chair.

Suspiciously the guard approached to check the bonds. As soon as he was in reach, Mike grabbed him and threw him neatly over his head in a classic judo throw.

Pausing only to make sure that the man had been knocked out by the fall, Mike crept cautiously from the hut.

It had taken the Doctor quite some time to choose the equipment he needed from the Prison Workshop, and an even longer time to assemble it to his satisfaction.

He had transferred the lot to a warder's office close to the Process Chamber, where he was engaged in checking it over once again. He was wearing a white coat, heavy gloves and a protective helmet with a transparent visor.

The results of the Doctor's efforts consisted of a huge electrical coil, in the form of a loop on the end of a very long length of wire, rather like a giant lasso.

The wire was connected to a square black box studded with controls, a rather special form of junction box, and this in turn was connected by yet more flex to the prison power supply.

The Master stood looking on, fuming with impatience.

'Doctor, you must hurry. If that thing starts moving again. . .'

'I am well aware of the importance of the situation,' said the Doctor calmly. He picked up the coil in one hand and the junction box in the other and carried them out into the main area of the prison, moving along the corridor and placing them as near to the Process Chamber as possible.

The Master watched in some puzzlement. 'May I ask what you intend to do, Doctor?'

'I'm going to try to throw this coil around that Machine in there – if I can get close enough without being killed.'

'I see – and what can I do to help?'

It was very clear from the Master's tone that any such help would be given from a safe distance.

The Doctor pointed to the junction box. There was a control panel, studded with lights and dials. 'I want you to operate these controls here. Switch them on to full power when I shout.'

The Master studied the box. 'Very ingenious. What does it do?'

'If all goes well, the box will set up an electric current in the coil – a current alternating on much the same frequency as the human brain.'

'And what will that do to the mind parasite?'

'I'm not sure – but I *hope* it will confuse the creature enough to inhibit its powers of movement.'

'I hope you're right, Doctor.'

'So do I,' said the Doctor grimly.

He picked up the coil and set off.

The Master took his place at the controls. 'Good luck, Doctor.'

The Doctor moved along the corridor, trailing flex behind him. He reached the door of the Process Chamber, opened it cautiously, and moved inside.

116

Sure enough, the Machine was back in place.

Perhaps the creature inside regarded the place as a kind of home, thought the Doctor. Perhaps it felt safe there.

The Doctor crept cautiously forward. He got quite close before the Machine reacted to his presence with its menacing, throbbing sound.

The sound built up with terrifying speed and suddenly the Doctor found that he was forcing himself forwards, struggling every inch of the way with the terrifying powers of the creature in the Machine.

Inside the transparent column the spongy mass was pulsating violently. It threw hallucinations at him in rapid succession; flames, Daleks, Cybermen and all the others. The electronic pulsing grew louder and louder. Somehow the Doctor managed to resist. He staggered closer and ever closer until at last, with a desperate heave, he was able to throw the coil over the Machine.

The Doctor backed away.

'Now!' he shouted over his shoulder.

Out in the corridor, the Master was working frantically on the junction box controls, trying to stabilise the power levels before the box overloaded and blew up. Warning lights flashed on the control panel, and the box began to smoke, growing hot to the touch. He managed it at last, and the lights flashed less wildly, and the smoke and heat died down.

In the Process Chamber the throbbing and pulsing of the Machine died down too.

The Doctor turned and walked wearily away.

He found the Master waiting in the corridor, Mailer beside him.

'My congratulations, Doctor,' said the Master generously.

'It won't hold it for long, you know,' warned the Doctor. 'That thing's *intelligent*. Soon it will work out what's happened and find a way to deal with the coil.'

'Then you'll have to think of something better, won't you? Mailer, take the Doctor back to his cell.'

The Master swept away.

Mailer jabbed the Doctor with his automatic. 'All right, come on, you.'

Jo looked up as Mailer shoved the Doctor back into the cell. The Doctor took a few steps and collapsed onto the bed.

Jo sat beside him, concerned. 'Are you all right, Doctor?'

'I'm fine, Jo,' said the Doctor wearily. 'Fine.'

'Did you fix the Machine?'

'Temporarily.'

'You look tired.'

'I am! Physically and mentally.' Wearily the Doctor began stripping off the protective clothing.

Jo had never seen the Doctor in such low spirits. 'Hey, how about some food?' she said brightly. 'Do you think they'll give us any?'

'I doubt it – not after what we did with the last lot!'

'We've had nothing all day – I'm starving,' protested Jo.

The Doctor smiled. 'Well, I suppose we shouldn't have hit them over the head with our breakfast!'

Jo jumped up. 'Breakfast. Wait a minute!'

She scrabbled about under the bed and emerged with two dusty pieces of cold toast. 'I knew they wouldn't bother to clean up.' She held one out to the Doctor, who recoiled.

'No thanks, Jo, you have it. I can go for quite a time without food, you know.'

'No, no, we'll share it,' insisted Jo. 'And there's still some water in the jug there.'

Jo poured out two glasses of water, gave a piece of toast to the Doctor.

She raised her glass. 'Cheers!'

'Cheers!' said the Doctor solemnly.

They settled down to their feast.

'Did I ever tell you about the time I was locked up in the Tower of London, Jo?' said the Doctor suddenly.

'No, I don't think so.'

'I shared a cell with a very strange chap called Walter Raleigh. He'd managed to get on the wrong side of Queen Elizabeth, you see – the first Queen Elizabeth. Anyway, he kept going on about some new vegetable he'd discovered, called the potato. Well, one day old Walter sat down and pointed a finger at me and said, "Doctor . . ."'

A large plain van drew up to the gates of Stangmoor Prison and its overalled and cloth-capped driver got out, and nodded cheerfully to the tough-looking guard.

'Morning, mate. Provisions!'

He was a tall man with a clipped, military moustache.

The guard glared at him. 'What?'

'Provisions,' repeated the driver patiently. 'Nosh! Food!'

'Back gate. You can't come in 'ere.'

'I can't go through the back gate either,' said the van driver reasonably. 'Van's too big.'

The guard shrugged. 'You'd better clear off then.'

'Now listen,' said the van driver persuasively. 'I've got a week's supply of food in there – *and* booze for the Governor. Am I supposed to go back and say you don't want it? They'll think you're barmy.'

The guard said, 'Hang about.' He spoke into his RT

set. 'Main gate, here. Er, Mr Mailer? I've got a big provision lorry here, food, booze, the lot. Do I let it in?'

A voice crackled from the RT. 'Yeah, okay. But I want him unloaded and out of here fast.'

The guard turned to the driver. 'Drive round the ring-road up to the main courtyard and unload. You'll find some blokes there to give you a hand. We've had a bit of trouble, see, and the Chief wants you out of here as soon as possible.'

'Don't worry, mate, less time I spend in there the better!'

The van driver got back in his van and revved up. It seemed to take rather a long time. While he was doing it, the rear doors of the van opened and three uniformed figures slid out.

The arched doorway was just big enough to admit the van and the three soldiers walked behind it unseen. Once inside, they jumped on the guards at the gate, knocking them out with swift efficiency.

The van trundled along the outer road that ringed the inner courtyard.

At a pre-arranged point it stopped, and half a dozen men, led by Sergeant Benton, scrambled out of the back and ran to a narrow gate set into the massive wall.

The gate was soon open, and the men disappeared in the narrow cleft in the wall. They emerged from the darkness onto a long flight of steps that ended in a tunnel set into yet another massive wall.

Ignoring the pounding in his head, Benton led his little party through the echoing darkness of the tunnel until they emerged into a little enclosed green. In front of them was another high stone wall – the rear wall of the inner courtyard.

'Right,' shouted Benton. 'Ropes and irons!'

Two of the men produced grappling hooks on the end of long nylon ropes. They hurled the hooks over the wall.

As soon as they were lodged fast, men began climbing upwards.

Meanwhile the provisions van drove up to a second checkpoint set in the inner wall. The main gate guard must have phoned ahead, because it was admitted without trouble.

The provisions van drove into the inner courtyard and stopped. Immediately it was surrounded by a little group of men, some dressed as warders, some still in their prison uniforms.

The cloth-capped driver jumped out of the cab and favoured the little group with a cheery wave. He went round to the back of the van and flung wide the doors, revealing not the expected supplies of food and drink but a tightly packed mass of UNIT soldiers, who leaped out of the van and piled into the astonished convicts, with fists and rifle-butts.

The van driver took a megaphone from the back of the van, strode into the centre of the courtyard and raised it to his lips. 'I am Brigadier Lethbridge-Stewart of UNIT. This prison is now in military hands . . .'

The effect of the Brigadier's carefully prepared little speech was rather spoiled when an armed convict high on the wall took a shot at him and hit the megaphone instead, smashing it from his hands.

The Brigadier dived, rolled over, and came up with his service automatic in his hands, shooting the prisoner neatly off the wall.

This was the signal for the battle to begin in earnest and the fighting, although brief, was bloody.

Armed convicts began appearing from the doorways that led into the courtyard, and running along the walkways on top of the high walls that surrounded it.

The Brigadier and his men used whatever cover they could find, in alcoves and stairways and behind parked vehicles – among them, the Brigadier noticed, the Doctor's beloved Bessie. Heaven help anyone who put a bullet in that!

As the Brigadier had predicted, the convicts, although surprisingly well supplied with weapons were untrained in their use. They blazed away wildly, wasting most of their shots, while the UNIT soldiers fought with deadly efficiency, using every scrap of cover and shooting only when they were sure of a hit.

Convicts tumbled screaming from the high walls, rolled down long staircases, collapsed wounded or dying on the cobbles.

What really turned the tables was the arrival of Benton and his party on the top of the rear wall. From there they soon swept the walkways clear of convicts. The remaining convicts' nerve broke and they began to fall back.

In the condemned cell, the Doctor and Jo were listening to the sounds of battle in amazement.

'It seems to be right *inside* the prison,' said Jo.

The Doctor nodded. 'The Brigadier probably used the old Trojan horse trick. I only hope he can gain complete control before Mailer starts killing the hostages.'

Since they themselves were hostages, Jo found it easy to agree.

'Yes, Doctor,' she said. 'So do I!'

The Brigadier looked round the courtyard, and realised that the battle was over. Most of the convicts were wounded or dead, the rest were beginning to surrender. He ran to the checkpoint and saw a UNIT lorry driving up the road from the main gate. Reinforcements had arrived.

Waving the lorry forward, the Brigadier yelled, 'Come on! I'm going to find the Doctor.'

He ran for one of the doors that led into the main building.

The cell door was flung open, to reveal Mailer. He was both angry and frightened.

'Come to give yourself up?' asked the Doctor affably.

'Shut up and listen. If you want to stay alive, do exactly as I say.'

'Well?'

'You two are going to walk out of here in front of me. Tell those mates of yours that either I get out or I chop you down.'

'They won't listen,' said Jo.

'Too bad for you if they don't,' said Mailer flatly.

'Now, come on.' He waved his automatic.

They walked through the deserted corridors in a little procession, first the Doctor, then Jo, then Mailer.

'No heroics,' warned Mailer. 'I only need one of you to get me out of here.'

They were descending a short metal staircase when Jo, with more courage than good sense, tried to be heroic after all.

She flung herself backwards at Mailer's legs, yelling, 'Now, Doctor!'

But the Doctor had no time to do anything – Mailer was too quick. He fell back onto the steps, one arm round Jo's throat, and his automatic still covering the Doctor.

'Too bad, Doctor,' he said softly. 'I warned you – I only need one of you . . .'

The Doctor watched helplessly. He saw Mailer's finger tighten on the trigger.

The Doctor braced himself – and heard the roar of an automatic pistol fired at close range . . .

14

The Reunion

To the Doctor's astonishment he did not however feel the impact of the bullet. Instead it was Mailer who fell, shot down by the Brigadier, who stood at the foot of the steps.

The Doctor drew a deep breath. 'Thank you, Brigadier. Do you think that just once you could manage to arrive *before* the nick of time?'

'I'm glad to see you too, Doctor. Are you all right, Miss Grant?'

'Yes, I'm fine.'

The Doctor looked in amusement at the Brigadier's overalls and cloth cap. 'I see you've changed your job!'

The Brigadier smiled. 'Rather an effective disguise, don't you think?' Clearly he had enjoyed his brief masquerade.

Sergeant Benton hurried in, beamed at the sight of the Doctor and Jo, wondered if he ought to salute the cloth-capped Brigadier, and decided he'd better play safe.

The Brigadier returned the salute, touching a hand to the rim of his cloth cap. 'Did you get the Master?'

'Sorry, sir, no sign of him. He seems to have got clean away.'

'What about the missile?' asked the Doctor.

'Not a sign of it, Doctor.'

The Brigadier looked aghast. 'Isn't it here?'

'No,' said the Doctor decisively. 'It most certainly is not.'

The Brigadier looked crestfallen. 'Oh! I rather assumed it was.'

'Well, Brigadier,' said the Doctor caustically, 'apart from losing the missile and the Master, you're doing very well.'

The Master had prepared his own escape route from the prison, and he was well on his way soon after the first shot was fired.

At this precise moment he was stepping out of his limousine outside the hangar.

The rocket, now assembled on its mobile launch-pad stood outside the hangar doors.

The Master's little team of mercenaries were standing by. At a nod from the Master, they operated the controls.

Slowly the great pointed nose of the rocket pointed skywards. It looked, thought the Master, like a great bird, poised and ready to fly.

The Doctor was pacing up and down the Governor's office.

'I tell you, Brigadier, the Master has got to be found.'

The Brigadier, now back in uniform, was studying a map. 'I happen to be rather more concerned with finding that missile, Doctor.'

'Surely it comes to the same thing – '

Sergeant Benton came in and saluted. 'Excuse me, sir, everything in the Prison is pretty well back to normal. Convicts are back in their cells, prison staff released and back in uniform and we're moving the wounded out now.'

'Very good, Sergeant.'

'We found this chap hiding in the medical wing, sir.' A UNIT soldier shoved Barnham forward. He'd managed to get himself dressed in prison uniform again, but he still wore the same confused, child-like expression. He looked uncertainly round the little group and smiled when he saw Jo.

'Well, lock him up with the others,' snapped the Brigadier.

'You leave him alone,' said Jo indignantly. She waved the UNIT soldier away. 'Come and sit down, Barnham.'

'There was all this shooting,' explained Barnham apologetically. 'I didn't know what to do . . .'

'It's all right,' said Jo soothingly. 'It's all over now, we'll look after you.' She looked accusingly at Benton. 'Has he been given any food?'

Despite the fact that he had recently been fully occupied in mopping up dangerous armed criminals, Benton looked apologetic. 'No, miss.'

'Well, don't just stand there, show me where I can get him something.'

'This way, miss,' said Benton meekly.

Jo followed him off, and Barnham sat obediently on his chair.

The Brigadier looked baffled. 'Who *is* that man, Doctor?'

'That's Barnham, the last man to undergo the Keller Process. You can see what it's made of him, he's got the mind of a child. Leave him to Jo, he trusts her.' The Doctor crossed over to the wall. 'Now, Brigadier, let's have a look at that map . . .'

Suddenly a voice crackled from the Brigadier's RT Set. 'Trap One to Greyhound. Trap One to Greyhound.'

The Doctor looked up. 'It's Captain Yates!'

The Brigadier snatched up the RT. 'Greyhound to Trap One. Is that you, Yates? Where are you?'

Mike Yates, weary, wounded but triumphant, was standing next to Major Cosgrove. 'I'm at the Mobile HQ, sir.'

'What happened to you?'

'A great deal, sir. I know where the Master has hidden the Thunderbolt.'

'Where?'

'In a hangar in a deserted airfield near Stanham, sir. They've got a crane, a launching pad, fake troops, the lot!'

The Brigadier looked triumphantly at the Doctor. 'Are you all right?'

Mike's cheerful voice came back over the RT. 'Bit bashed about, sir, but I might just survive.'

'Well done, Yates. All right, stay where you are. I'm on my way.'

The Brigadier swung round to the Doctor. 'No need to worry about the Master this time – we've got him!'

In the hangar hut, the Master was making final precise adjustments to the launch co-ordinates of the missile . . . and in the Process Chamber, the Keller Machine, forgotten for the moment, was beginning to throb angrily inside the restraining coil.

The Brigadier was busy briefing Benton before his own departure for the airfield. 'Right, you'll be in charge of Stangmoor Prison while I'm away, Benton. You can consider yourself acting Governor!' He waved Benton to the Governor's chair.

Rather gingerly, Benton sat down. 'Thank you, sir.'

'And Benton – don't get any delusions of grandeur, will you?'

The Brigadier strolled over to the Doctor who lay sprawled in an armchair, staring into space.

'Well, that just about wraps it up, Doctor.'

'Does it?'

'Major Cosgrove is throwing a cordon around that hangar right now. I'll join him at the Mobile HQ and we'll move in and mop up.'

'You may not find the Master all that easy to mop up,' grumbled the Doctor.

'Oh I don't anticipate much trouble, Doctor.'

'He's got that nerve gas missile, remember. He can aim it at London – or any city in Europe, come to that.'

'Don't worry, he isn't going to get the chance. Aren't you coming with us?'

'No, not for the moment. I've got to find a way of destroying that Machine of his. If I step up the voltage in those coils . . .' The Doctor began muttering obstruse calculations to himself.

The Brigadier said, 'Well, I'll leave the Machine to you, Doctor – and you can leave the Master to me!'

The throbbing of the box was reaching a crescendo now and the restraining coil was red hot and sending off smoke and flame. An energy-storm whirled through the Process Chamber, sending chairs and tables flying through the air.

Suddenly the junction box in the corridor exploded. The console blew up and the coil disintegrated in a shower of sparks.

The Machine disappeared.

Two Prison officers, newly restored to freedom and authority were walking along the corridor, enjoying things being more or less back to normal.

They stopped in astonishment at the sight of the exploded, still-smoking junction box.

Suddenly the Machine materialised in front of them, throbbing hungrily.

A blood-red shimmering filled the air as it sucked the life force from them in one fearful surge of power.

The Doctor was still muttering calculations as Jo came back into the Governor's office with a tray on which was a bowl of tomato soup.

'Here you are, Barnham, some nice hot soup for you,' she said encouragingly. 'Eat it all up.'

Barnham took the soup. 'Thank you, miss.' Obediently he began to eat.

'That's it,' said the Doctor suddenly. 'I think that might just do it!'

He jumped to his feet and dashed out.

As always, Jo's insatiable curiosity got the better of her. 'Wait for me, Doctor,' she called and ran out after him.

Barnham looked on in mild astonishment.

Benton's phone rang. 'Sergeant, sorry, Acting Governor Benton.'

'It's Doctor Summers here. I was wondering if those extra medical supplies had arrived?'

'Medical supplies? Hang on, Doctor Summers, I'll check.'

Benton began sorting through the file of receipts and requisitions on his desk.

Suddenly he became aware of Barnham hovering over him. 'What do you think you're doing mate?'

'Doctor Summers,' said Barnham happily.

'You what?'

'I'd like to talk to Doctor Summers.'

Benton found the paper he was looking for. 'You go and talk to whoever you like mate,' he said absently. He picked up the phone. 'Doctor Summers? They're here all right. Should be on their way over to you now.'

By the time Benton had finished his conversation and put the phone down Barnham had wandered off.

Jo and the Doctor looked down at the exploded junction box and the two crumpled bodies.

'Oh no!' whispered the Doctor. 'That thing's escaped again.'

'But how?'

'It must have stored up all its energy until it had enough power to fuse the circuits.'

Which meant that it would be hungry again, thought the Doctor. He got up and walked slowly towards the Process Chamber, as if dreading what he might find.

'Be careful, Doctor,' called Jo and hurried after him.

They stood in the doorway of the Process Chamber, looking round in horror at the wrecked room. The place was a total shambles, smashed furniture and shattered equipment scattered everywhere.

'What happened?' whispered Jo.

'It's stronger than ever now, Jo. How on earth am I going to stop it?'

Barnham came wandering along the corridor.

He stopped for a moment staring in distress at the two bodies. Then, as if drawn by some compulsion, he made his way towards the Process Chamber.

'Will you be able to set up that thing with the coils again?' asked Jo.

The Doctor shook his head despairingly. 'No, that would never work twice. The thing's too intelligent. It would probably kill me before I got near it.'

Suddenly they heard the familiar throbbing noise – and the Keller Machine materialised on the table before them.

They could feel its pull now, and Jo in particular seemed transfixed. She began taking stumbling steps towards the box.

The Doctor tried to pull her back, and found to his horror that he couldn't move. The mind parasite had become too strong for him.

Jo stumbled nearer the Machine . . .

15

The Mind of Evil

Suddenly the throbbing of the Machine died down.

The Doctor pulled Jo back – and Barnham stumbled into the room.

'Get back, Barnham,' shouted the Doctor. 'Don't come in!'

Barnham stared dazedly at him, and came on into the room. 'I had to come . . . then I heard this noise.'

As he came closer, the throbbing of the Machine died down completely.

'It's stopped,' whispered Jo.

Barnham looked round the room. 'I remember this place. Something happened to me here. Something terrible.'

Frightened, Barnham backed away – and as he retreated towards the door, the terrible throbbing began again.

A wonderful, incredible idea came to the Doctor's mind. 'Barnham, *don't* go,' he called.

Frightened Barnham still backed away.

The throbbing grew louder.

'Barnham, it's all right!' called the Doctor. 'Come back here, please. It can't hurt you *and while you're here it can't hurt us!*'

Barnham advanced slowly into the room. The throbbing of the Machine died away again.

The Doctor took Barnham's arm. 'That's right, this

way.' He picked up an overturned chair, set it up close to the Machine and sat Barnham down on it. 'That's right, old chap, you sit there.'

Jo saw that Barnham was right next to the Machine – and the Machine was silent, dead.

'I don't understand, Doctor. Why?'

The Doctor was overjoyed. 'Eureka! Don't you see, Jo, the Mind of Evil. The creature in the box *feeds* on the evil pulses in the mind.'

'And Barnham doesn't have any!'

'Exactly! The Machine extracted them all. Now, somehow or other the effect of Barnham's mind acts as a screen, it neutralises the mind parasite. As long as Barnham's here, we're safe!'

Captain Yates and Major Cosgrove rose, as the Brigadier strode briskly into the Mobile HQ.

'Good afternoon, Major Cosgrove. How are you, Captain Yates?'

Mike Yates had had a chance to clean himself up, and he had undergone the attention of a UNIT medical orderly. His right arm was in a sling but otherwise he was pretty much himself again.

'Recovering rapidly, sir,' he said cheerfully.

'Good. Well sit down both of you. How's it going, Major?'

'Fine sir – and there's excellent news. I've checked with the Ministry of Defence and it appears that Thunderbolt is equipped with an abort mechanism. As soon as it's in go condition – we can blow it up any time.'

The Brigadier said happily, 'So, if the Master threatens to launch the missile – we simply blow it up from here?'

'Exactly, sir.'

The Doctor had taken the dome from the top of the Machine and he and Jo were looking in horror at the creature beneath. Not that it was all that impressive. It was a lump of blue, spongy substance, not unlike a brain itself in appearance, with a sort of central nucleus that just might have been an eye. Yet somehow it radiated evil.

'Can't you kill it now, Doctor?' asked Jo.

'The creature is incredibly resilient. It would take an atomic explosion to destroy it completely. Or an enormous charge of electricity. Yes, that's it!' The Doctor made for the door. 'You and Barnham wait here. I've got to go and see Sergeant Benton.'

Jo shuddered, but said bravely, 'All right.'

The Doctor put a hand on Barnham's shoulder. 'Barnham, old chap, listen to me. Will you stay here with Jo till I get back? It's important.'

'I'm frightened,' said Barnham piteously. 'It's evil.'

'I'll be as quick as I can,' said the Doctor. 'Look after him, Jo.'

The Doctor hurried away.

Jo smiled encouragingly at Barnham, trying to distract him from the horror in the Machine.

'What's your first name?' she asked. 'I don't think you ever told me . . .'

The Doctor was showering a baffled Benton with orders and instructions. 'Now you're sure you've got all that, Sergeant?'

'I think so, Doctor. Extra heavy-duty cable, arrangements with the National Electricity Grid for a massive power surge on command. I'll get on to it right away.'

'Please do,' urged the Doctor. 'It's all very urgent.'

'It's going to take quite a bit of organising . . .'

'I don't doubt it,' said the Doctor impatiently. 'Nevertheless, please do your best.'

Benton reached for his telephone but it rang as he put his hand on it. He picked it up. 'Acting Governor Benton.'

A deep, puzzled voice said, 'I *beg* your pardon?'

'This is Stangmoor Prison. Acting Governor Benton speaking.'

'I see,' said the voice. 'Is the Doctor available by any chance?'

'I'll see, sir. Who's calling?'

'Oh, just tell him it's an old friend.'

Benton passed the phone to the Doctor. 'For you, Doctor. Says it's an old friend.'

The Doctor took the phone. 'Hello?'

'Ah, Doctor,' said a familiar voice. 'I gather that the tables have been turned at Stangmoor?'

'You have gathered correctly,' said the Doctor acidly. 'Let me tell you exactly what's been going on . . .'

Jo and Barnham had long ago run out of conversation. They were sitting tensely, trying not to look at the creature in the Machine when Doctor Summers burst into the room.

'Jo, what the devil do you think you're doing? And you, Barnham! I've been looking for you, everywhere. I told you to stay in the Medical Wing. Come on!'

'Doctor Summers, he *can't* go,' pleaded Jo. 'We've *got* to stay by the Machine.'

'But you'll get yourselves killed.'

'We can't leave,' said Jo obstinately.

'Look, Jo, you know Barnham isn't really well yet – and you know that thing is dangerous.' He turned to Barnham. 'Come on, now.'

Barnham looked worriedly from one to the other. 'Please, I can't . . . my head's hurting . . .'

As Barnham's concentration was weakened, the Machine began a low angry throbbing, and the strange sponge-like substance began to pulsate.

Doctor Summers stared at it in horror. 'That thing – it's alive!'

'That's right,' said Jo fiercely. 'And unless Barnham

134

stays here – *undisturbed* – it will break loose and kill us all!'

The Doctor was concluding his account of recent events at Stangmoor. 'So you've lost, you see,' he concluded. 'The prison is in our hands, and UNIT has you surrounded. Now, in the light of present circumstances, do you still intend to fire that missile at London?'

'I most certainly do, Doctor. And later, when this miserable planet is in ruins, I shall take over.'

'Aren't you forgetting something?'

'Am I, Doctor? What?'

'The dematerialisation circuit I took from your TARDIS. You can never leave Earth without it.'

On a previous encounter, the Doctor had removed the vital dematerialisation circuit from the Master's TARDIS – which was why the Master, like the Doctor, was currently stranded on Earth.

There was a long silence.

'Are you offering me a deal, Doctor?'

'I am. Hand over that rocket and I'll give you back your dematerialisation circuit.'

'How very generous of you.'

'You can leave Earth and leave us in peace. Go and make trouble somewhere else.'

There was another pause.

'Well,' said the Doctor impatiently. 'What do you say?'

'Very well. You will bring the circuit to me at the hangar, Doctor. You, and you alone. Any sign of treachery, any interference from your UNIT friends and I shall launch the missile immediately.'

The Doctor heard a click as the phone was put down at the other end.

The Doctor turned to Benton. 'Can you contact the Brigadier for me?'

135

'Yes, Doctor. He'll be at the Mobile HQ by now.'

'Then get me on to him at once. He's got to cancel that attack.'

Doctor Summers was reluctantly preparing to leave the Process Chamber. 'If you're sure I can't do anything?'

'No, really,' Jo liked Doctor Summers, but she was wishing desperately that he would just go, before he distracted Barnham further.

'Very well. I've got a lot of wounded men to look after. I'll be in the Medical Wing if you need me. Look after him, Jo – and look after yourself.' He patted Barnham on the shoulder. 'Mind you do exactly as Miss Grant says.'

Doctor Summers hurried away.

Jo looked worriedly at Barnham. 'How are you feeling now?'

'I'm tired, but I'm all right.'

'Try and concentrate on keeping calm. It won't be much longer . . .'

The Doctor said, 'Don't you understand, Brigadier? You mustn't go anywhere near the Master. If he catches sight of a uniform, he'll fire that missile immediately.'

The Brigadier's voice was too confident for the Doctor's liking. 'Don't you worry, Doctor. Leave everything to us.'

'Will you do as I ask?'

'We'll cancel the attack, and I'll send a despatch rider to HQ for your circuit – just in case.'

'What do you mean, just in case? Persuading him to make that exchange is our only chance!'

'Oh, I don't think so, Doctor. There are other ways to deal with him.'

'Now don't do anything stupid, Brigadier. The Master means what he says.'

The Brigadier remained infuriatingly cheerful. 'Don't you worry, Doctor. Over and out.'

136

'Lethbridge-Stewart, wait!' shouted the Doctor. But the RT was dead.

The Brigadier *was* feeling rather pleased with himself. The Doctor had been trying to deal with the Master for goodness knows how many years – and now *he* was about to do it for him. He turned to Major Cosgrove. 'I want you to get on to the Missile Control people. Confirm that they're to maintain radio link with us, and explode the missile when I give the word.'

'Right away, sir.'

'Captain Yates, you'll be in charge of the evacuation. I want the area around that hangar completely cleared within a ten-mile radius.'

'Right, sir.'

Cosgrove picked up the RT. 'Trap One to Missile Control . . .'

The Doctor was pacing about the Process Chamber.

Barnham sat with his hands on his knees, and the Machine was still.

'I don't see why you're so upset, Doctor,' said Jo. 'If you give him back the circuit, and he hands over the missile. . .'

The Doctor sighed. 'You don't understand, do you Jo? Once he gets that circuit back he's free to roam through Time and Space. We'd never catch him.'

Jo could hear the yearning in the Doctor's voice. Suddenly she realised what it would mean to him to give the Master his freedom, while he himself remained an exile.

Sadly Jo said, 'You'll just have to give in, Doctor. The Master's got the missile, and all we've got is this wretched Machine.'

'There's no need to point out the obvious, Jo – ' The Doctor broke off, staring hard at her. '*What* did you say?'

137

'I said all we've got is the Machine.'

'That's it! That's the answer! We've got the Machine – and we've also got our friend Barnham.'

Barnham looked puzzled. 'I don't understand.'

The Doctor rubbed his hands. 'With a little help from you, old chap, we're going to destroy this Machine and the Master – both at the same time.'

The Master was busy dismantling the abort circuit on the missile control console. He smiled. 'Just in case anyone tries to be clever . . .'

To everyone's relief the dome had been put back on the Keller Machine, concealing the mind parasite inside.

Benton hurried into the Process Chamber. 'Everything's laid on, Doctor.'

'Thank you, Sergeant. Are you ready, Barnham? Do you understand what to do?'

'I think so. . .'

Reluctantly, Barnham approached the Machine. It began throbbing angrily.

'Don't worry, it can't hurt *you*,' said Jo encouragingly.

Screwing up his courage, Barnham seized the Machine and lifted it up. The throbbing stopped immediately.

'Well done, old chap,' said the Doctor. 'Just remember, whatever you do, don't drop it. Now then, off we go. Easy does it, that's the idea.'

Slowly Barnham carried the box towards the door. The others followed.

When the Doctor arrived at the Mobile HQ followed by his entourage, he found the Brigadier distinctly crestfallen.

'We tried to explode the missile on the ground with the abort circuit Doctor, but nothing happened.'

'Well, what did you expect?' said the Doctor scornfully. 'The Master may be a scoundrel, but he is a scientist. He'll have disconnected the abort mechanism.'

'Which means there's only one thing for it, Doctor. You'll have to go through with your deal and give him back his wretched circuit.'

'Is it here?'

The Brigadier looked at Major Cosgrove who said calmly, 'Just arrived, sir.' He handed the Doctor a small sealed packet.

The Doctor ripped it open and took out a little box. Inside it was the Master's dematerialisation circuit, a complicated little affair that looked vaguely like the model of an atom. The Doctor looked sadly at it.

'I know how you feel, Doctor,' said the Brigadier sympathetically. 'I hate to see the Master escape as much as you do.'

'It's *where* he'll escape to that worries me. What right have we to turn him lose on some other planet?'

'Well, unless you've got a better plan, I see no alternative.'

'My dear Brigadier, of course I've got a better plan. Just you listen to me . . .'

The Doctor drove the Black Maria along the path towards the hangar, where the Master stood waiting by his missile. In the back sat Barnham, desperately clutching the Machine, with Jo beside him.

The Master looked suspicious as the Black Maria drove up to him.

Suddenly there was a gun in his hand. 'A very strange form of transport, Doctor. I hope you're not going to try anything silly.'

'No, of course not. It's just that Bessie's broken down.'

'Bessie?'

The Doctor made driving motions with his hands.

'You know, Bessie!'

Jo opened the rear door of the Black Maria and she and Barnham began a cautious descent.

They could hear the Master's voice. 'I think I should warn you Doctor that my – ' the Master mimicked the Doctor's driving movement '– is all primed and ready to fire.'

The Doctor looked up at the towering bulk of the missile like a tourist admiring the Eiffel Tower. 'That's very clever. My word, you have done well. Shall we get on with it?'

'Did you bring the circuit with you?'

'Ah, yes – here.'

The Doctor slipped a little box from his pocket, and opened the lid to reveal the circuit.

The Master's eyes gleamed. 'May I examine it?'

'How do I know you won't take the circuit and fire the missile anyway?'

'You don't. Just this once, Doctor, you'll have to trust me.'

The Master held out his hand.

16

The Farewell

For a moment no one moved or spoke.

Then the Doctor said slowly. 'Trust you? No – I don't think so.'

Jo and Barnham appeared round the side of the Black Maria.

'Now, Doctor,' shouted Jo.

Barnham put the Machine down as close to the Master as he dared. The Master stared at it in horror – and the Doctor kicked the gun from the Master's hand.

The Master leaped upon him and for a moment the two Time Lords grappled furiously.

Jo grabbed Barnham's hand and dragged him towards the hangar.

Released from the restraint of Barnham's presence, the Machine began throbbing furiously.

With a final desperate heave, the Doctor threw the Master bodily towards the Machine, then turned and sprinted for the hangar office.

The Master tried to get to his feet and follow, but by now the Machine was fully aroused. It began drawing the Master towards it, inflamed no doubt by the super-abundance of evil in his mind . . .

The Master used every atom of his will to resist. He was poised, locked, trapped in an almost perfect balance between his will and the strength of the Machine.

But the Machine was stronger. The Master writhed in agony as the Machine forced him to crawl towards it.

Jo Grant was talking into her RT. 'Hello, Brigadier, Jo Grant here. Over.'

The Brigadier's voice crackled back. 'Hello, Miss Grant, we read you. Over.'

'The Doctor is working on the missile abort circuit. Stand by for abort instructions, over.'

'Well done, Miss Grant. Greyhound to Windmill 342. Come in to land. I say again, come in to land.'

From somewhere overhead, Jo heard the drone of a UNIT helicopter.

The Doctor meanwhile was busy at the console, reinstating the abort circuit. Fortunately the Master had just removed it, and not destroyed it.

With the circuit in place, the Doctor finished the last few connections and ran from the hut. 'Right, Jo.'

Jo spoke into the RT. 'We're on our way!'

The helicopter touched down just as Jo, Barnham and the Doctor ran from the hangar towards it.

Face twisted in agony, the Master was using the last remnants of his strength to resist the power of the Machine.

The Doctor and Jo gave him a wide berth on their way to the helicopter, but Barnham couldn't bear to see anyone in pain, not even the Master. He stopped to help.

It was a fatal mistake. Barnham's nearness damped down the power of the Machine sufficiently for the Master to break free.

Knocking Barnham aside, the Master leaped into the driving seat of the Black Maria and sped across the tarmac.

It was unfortunate that Barnham stumbled into his way.

The Doctor and Jo turned just in time to see the Black Maria slam into Barnham, smashing him to the tarmac, and then disappear into the distance.

Jo and the Doctor ran back to Barnham, who lay twisted and still. Quickly the Doctor examined him. 'He's dead, Jo.' Jo's eyes filled with tears.

The Doctor grabbed her hand, and pulled her back towards the helicopter. They clambered inside and with a roar of its rotors the helicopter took off.

In the Mobile HQ, Major Cosgrove was saying calmly, 'Twenty seconds.'

The Brigadier took up the countdown. 'Ten . . . nine . . . eight . . . seven . . . six . . . five . . . four . . . three . . . two . . . one – abort.'

The Doctor and Jo glanced down from the fast-climbing helicopter. They were just in time to see the rocket, the hangar and the Machine disappear in smoke and flames.

The helicopter soared upwards above the clouds.

The atmosphere in the Governor's office was far from jubilant.

'We took Barnham there to help us, Doctor,' insisted Jo. 'We should never have left him.'

'I know,' said the Doctor sharply. 'How do you think I feel about it?'

Jo looked into his grimly-set face and realised that his distress was just as great as her own.

'I'm sorry,' she said softly.

The Doctor nodded. 'Here, have some coffee.'

The Brigadier did his best to cheer them up. 'Well, at least we're rid of the Keller Machine – and the Master.'

'The creature in the Machine must have been killed in the explosion,' agreed the Doctor. 'But I'm not so sure about the Master.'

The Brigadier said, 'Well, even if he wasn't killed, he can't get far. You've still got the circuit – haven't you Doctor?'

The Doctor felt in his pockets, casually at first then with increasing alarm. 'It's gone! I must have lost it in my scuffle with the Master.'

'It was probably destroyed in the explosion, Doctor,' said the Brigadier.

'Supposing it wasn't! Supposing the Master found it?'

The telephone rang.

Benton picked it up. 'Hello, yes, who is it?' He passed the phone to the Doctor. 'It's for you.'

'The Master!' said the Doctor grimly.

And indeed it was. 'I was afraid you might be worried about me, Doctor, so I called to let you know I'm alive and well.'

'I'm extremely sorry to hear that!'

The Master laughed. 'I managed to reach the safety of my TARDIS – now in perfect working order again – thanks to your generosity, Doctor.'

So, the Master *had* found the circuit after all, thought the Doctor. He did his best to put a brave face on it. 'I hope that means we've seen the last of you?'

The Master's voice vibrated with anger. 'For some little time, Doctor. But rest assured – one day I shall destroy this miserable planet – and you with it.' The Master laughed. 'Goodbye, Doctor.' He paused. 'Oh, and Doctor – enjoy your exile!'

The Doctor slammed down the phone, cutting off the sound of the Master's mocking laughter.

'What did he say?' asked Jo.

'Oh, the usual threats!'

'Never mind, Doctor,' said Jo consolingly. 'You've beaten him.'

'Have I? His TARDIS is working again. He can go when and where he pleases. And I'm trapped on Earth,' said the Doctor accusingly. 'With *you*, Brigadier!'